A HIGHWAYMAN CAME RIDING

A Highwayman Came Riding

Joan Smith

ISIS

LARGE PRINT

Oxford

First published in Great Britain 2005
by
Robert Hale Ltd.

Published in Large Print 2006 by ISIS Publishing Ltd.,
7 Centremead, Osney Mead, Oxford OX2 0ES
by arrangement with
Robert Hale Ltd.

British Library Cataloguing in Publication Data
Smith, Joan, 1953–
   A highwayman came riding. – Large print ed.
   1. Brigands and robbers – England – Fiction
   2. Love stories
   3. Large type books
   I. Title
   813.5'4 [F]

ISBN 0–7531–7598–3 (hb)
ISBN 0–7531–7599–1 (pb)

Printed and bound in Great Britain by
T. J. International Ltd., Padstow, Cornwall

CHAPTER
ONE

Marianne's head rested on her shoulder as the carriage jogged eastward through the waning afternoon light. Her eyes were closed, but she was not sleeping. It was a long journey from Bath to London. One hundred miles, according to the duchess. Eighty of those miles had been accomplished over the past two days. Her Grace traveled at a pace that made a snail look like an Olympic runner. Frequent stops were required to rest her weary, noble bones. With her weak heart, she ought not to be undertaking such a strenuous journey, but the marriage of her great-granddaughter to a duke's eldest son, to be celebrated with all pomp in St. George's of Hanover Square, was too grand an occasion to forgo.

There was no truth to the rumor running around Bath that she was really going because the Prince of Wales (and two of his sisters) were to attend. She had had a *tendre* for him three decades ago when he was a mere stripling, but he was now too old to incite her to passion. She still had a colt's tooth in her head. At eighty-two, she preferred younger, more attractive gentlemen than the portly Prince Regent.

She would normally have stopped her journey long before dusk but with a free night's lodging only ten miles away, the clutch-fisted old lady had insisted on continuing to Chertsey, despite her coachman's warning of the danger of highwaymen. Echoes of that unsettling conversation lingered in Marianne's mind as the ancient hard-sprung carriage jogged along with the wind soughing dolefully through the trees.

"You are thinking of the diamonds I plan to wear to Augusta's wedding," had been Her Grace's reply to Beeton's warning. "It is true the necklace would be a strong temptation to such villains, but no one knows I am carrying it. I put about word in Bath that my nephew Clarence had taken the necklace to London a week ago. That is the way to foil those sly rogues. They listen at taverns to learn when such precious cargo as my diamonds will be on the road."

"'Twas the strawberry leaves on the panel of your coach I was thinking of, Your Grace. That will be a lure to the scamps," Beeton explained. "It's this area near London where they ply their trade."

"That is why you and the postilion are carrying pistols, Beeton," Her Grace replied. "Don't hesitate to use 'em if we are attacked. This menace of highwaymen has been greatly exaggerated. We have gone eighty miles with no more trouble than that broken axle at Farnborough. I do not hold you responsible for it, Beeton, even if I did tell you to give the rig a thorough overhaul before we left. Anyone can make a mistake. Just drive quickly, and we shall be at Chertsey before nightfall. No sane scamp would attack before dark."

As the autumn shadows were already lengthening at five o'clock, Beeton could not think they would be at

Chertsey before dark, but he knew well enough the futility of arguing with his mistress when her chosen course would save her a penny. Penny wise, pound foolish, that was her way. She should be accompanied by a few mounted footmen, but the cost of feeding the nags and paying for a change of horses prevented it. It was only Tom, the postilion, who rode with them, and his gun was an ancient fowling piece that hadn't been fired in twenty years.

The resigned look Beeton cast on Miss Harkness was his only further objection. Her Grace's intractable nature was well known to all her servants, and though Marianne was a lady, she was paid a meager wage and was a servant in all but name. Her official title was companion. Her actual role was that of nurse, dresser, and general dogsbody to the demanding old dame.

Marianne had known better times, but after five years those halcyon days with her carefree parents were becoming a dim memory. Her mama had died of consumption when Marianne was sixteen. Her papa had drunk himself into the grave within the year, after first gambling away his fortune. Marianne had written the news to various members of her family in hopes of finding a home with one of them. She told herself the letters that arrived, one after another, complaining of hard times and families that were already too large, were true and tried to believe it. It was her Aunt Victoria who had written to the Duchess of Bixley, a connection of the family, recommending Marianne as a companion.

Despite the duchess's nipcheese ways and sharp tongue, Marianne was grateful to her. She had learned how to handle the dame with the proper degree of deference and common sense the old lady liked. Her Grace did not really care for what she called doormats.

Life at Bath, where the duchess had retired to a mansion upon her husband's death a decade before, was not particularly difficult, but it was extremely boring for a young lady who ought to have been making her debut, meeting beaux, and nabbing a husband. When Her Grace had had that heart attack last year, a new worry had been added to Marianne's shoulders. At eighty-two, the old dame could not live much longer. What would become of Marianne when the duchess died?

She had hopes that this trip to London might throw her into the path of some undemanding gentleman who required a wife. Although she knew it was a vicar, a schoolmaster, or some such genteel nonentity she might possibly attract, she could at least enjoy dreaming of someone more dashing. Without undue modesty, she accepted that she was no Incomparable. She was of average size, with brown hair that she wore drawn back from a high brow. Her eyes, she thought, were her best feature, though no gentleman had ever likened them to sapphires or even cornflowers. As she sank into a doze, a vision of her knight in shining armor rose up in her mind to beguile the idle hours.

She was caught totally off guard when the duchess reached out and gave her elbow a jostle. "Psst. Wake up, Marianne. Do you not hear it?"

Marianne shook herself to attention and listened to what sounded at first like thunder. But as she listened more closely, the sound took on a regular rhythm. Hoofbeats! The sound of the galloping hoofbeats behind them grew louder, more ominous, overriding the pounding of her heart. No one rode at such a breakneck speed unless he was either giving chase or being chased. She could discern no softer echo of hoofbeats following the louder, closer ones. "A highwayman!" she gasped.

"Let down the window and holler to Beeton, in case he has not heard it." With trembling fingers, Marianne applied herself to the task. "Hurry, child! Thank God I have secured the diamonds. I'll give him this set of fishpaste pearls I wore especially in case of attack. Let me do the talking."

It was soon evident that Beeton had indeed heard their attacker. The first shot that rang out came from the driver's seat. It was quickly followed by an answering shot from behind. The horses, accustomed to the polite manner of valetudinarian Bath, panicked and bolted.

"Egad, he's killed Beeton!" Her Grace cried. "Beeton would never let the team get away from him."

Marianne froze in fear. And all the time the hoofbeats came pounding louder, nearer. What would the highwayman do when the duchess handed him those cheap pearls that would not fool a child? Would he rip the gown from the old woman's bony chest and find the diamonds concealed beneath? What would he do when he discovered Marianne had nothing but a couple of guineas to give him? Would he shoot her? Her throat was dry and aching.

Before she could think of any means of escape, the highwayman was alongside them. Until that moment, she hadn't realized their carriage had stopped. Beeton was not dead, or if he was, Tom had got control of the team. The black halfmask that appeared at the window was infinitely menacing. The mouth and strong jaw below it were set in a grim line. The man wore a black slouch hat pulled low over his forehead, revealing the glitter of eyes that hardly looked human.

She heard the fateful words so often heard in imagination since setting out on this trip: "Stand and deliver," uttered in a voice of deadly calm. Her blood seemed to turn to ice in her veins. She could not stand if her life depended on it. When the voice spoke again, it was edged with impatience. "Out of the carriage, now!"

Moving as one in a trance, she turned the handle and trembled out into the dusky light, unaware of the stark, black branches of trees that looked like giant skeletal fingers clawing at the pewter sky. She had not realized it was so windy out. A cold north wind snatched at her mantle, whipping it about her knees. The duchess came out behind her, puffing with fear and fatigue and indignation. The highwayman leveled his gun at the duchess's chest. Without turning his head, he called "Miguel," and another rider appeared from the front of the carriage. He wore the same style of mask and hat as the first highwayman and also carried a pistol. "You've taken care of the men?"

6

"I have, Cap'n."

Marianne looked over his shoulder and saw Beeton and Tom lying on the ground, facedown, their hands tied behind their backs.

"The ladies have a donation for you," the first highwayman said in a perfectly pleasant voice. A cultured voice, Marianne noticed. But then, one heard that many of the scamps were well-born.

"But dash it, Cap'n, they're *ladies*!" the second man said. His voice was rougher. Odd that the servant, for so he appeared to be, should have the instincts of a gentleman. "They ain't —"

His cohort's voice cut him off in mid-speech. "A brace of noble dames, if I am not mistaken," he said. As he spoke, he reached out and fingered the duchess's pearls — and laughed. A touch was all it took for him to realize they were fakes. "What are we wearing beneath our gown?" he asked in a mocking voice. He did not rip the duchess's gown off. He rather gently moved his left hand to the back of her neck, fumbled a moment, and lifted off her diamond necklace. It dangled from his fingers, glowing and sparkling dully in the wan light. "A handsome bauble," he allowed, and dropped it into his pocket while the duchess looked on, speechless, for once.

The highwayman turned his attention to Marianne. "And you, milady?"

Marianne wordlessly handed him her reticule. He handed it to his assistant, who rummaged inside it. "Two guineas," Miguel said, and handed the reticule back to her without taking the money. She noticed he moved his arm stiffly, as if it hurt.

The other highwayman, the one who seemed to be in charge, studied Marianne with that menacing, glittering eye. "You travel light," he said. Something in his tone suggested disbelief. With his left hand, he reached out and unfastened her cloak as calmly as if he were her dresser and not a criminal who planned to rob her. Marianne hardly knew what to think. Did he plan to molest her? His hand went to her throat. She felt his warm fingers inside her collar. They moved intimately, stroking her skin in a leisurely manner as they continued down a few inches until they rested on the swell of her bosom. She didn't speak. She hardly dared breathe or imagine what liberty he would take next. His fingers brushed toward the back of her neck. Finding no concealed necklace, they returned to the front of her gown and settled on the oval cameo at her collar.

"A keepsake?" he asked.

"Y-yes," she stammered. "From my mama."

"Let her keep it!" the duchess said. As she began to recover from her first shock, her imperative manner returned. "It has no monetary value. There are five guineas in my reticule. Take them, and leave the child her memento."

Marianne was surprised and touched by the old lady's gesture — and by her bravery.

The highwayman did not reply with words, but he withdrew his hand without taking the cameo. "Your names, ladies?" he asked.

The duchess puffed out her chest and announced, "I am the Duchess of Bixley, and this is my companion."

The highwayman's eyes never left Marianne's face. She felt hypnotized by their brilliant glitter. "You have a name, ma'am?"

"She is Miss Harkness. And now if you are quite through with us, may we continue on our way, villain?"

A mocking smile curved the highwayman's lips. "Did no one ever tell you it is not nice to call names, Your Grace? For that, you shall pay a forfeit. That ring on your left hand — an emerald, is it? — the one you have been trying to conceal? I'll have it."

"You'll not!" she cried. "That ring was a gift from Queen Charlotte, a token of the Season I spent as one of her ladies-in-waiting."

"Hard earned, no doubt, but you must be taught a lesson."

The duchess's reply was spat out in an angry hiss. "I do not take lessons from villains!"

"No more you should, but you shall take one from me, madame!" On this angry retort, he reached out to seize her left hand. His pistol was in his right hand. The duchess made a snatch for it. Marianne leapt to prevent the man from shooting the duchess. In the melee, the pistol went off. The duchess collapsed in a heap on the ground. Marianne rushed to her side to render assistance.

Miguel and the other highwayman exchanged a startled look.

"Good God, Captain! You've killed the old malkin!" Miguel exclaimed.

CHAPTER
TWO

Marianne fell to her knees, trying to resuscitate her mistress. "Brandy. Do you have brandy?" she asked the highwayman who was called Captain. She saw no wound, no blood. Her heart, then.

The highwayman replied, "Not I. Miguel, do you have — good God! *You've* been shot as well."

"Just a scratch, Cap'n," he said in a weak voice and, clutching his arm, promptly fainted dead away.

"There's wine in the carriage. Get it," Marianne said. In the agitation of the moment, with fear of the duchess's death staring them in the face, she spoke without thinking of the consequences. She was familiar with her mistress's condition and took charge automatically. The captain rushed to the carriage and returned with the bottle of wine. It had been opened and recorked. There was half a bottle left. Marianne propped up the duchess's head and he held the bottle to her lips. The wine dribbled down her chin. "It's her heart," she explained.

It was like a blow to the stomach to see the proud dame reduced to the drooling of a baby. And it was all the fault of this man who would rather rob helpless old ladies than do an honest day's work. She turned on him in fury. "She's dead! You've killed her. Murderer. I'll see you dance from the gibbet for this!"

When she glanced over her shoulder and saw again that menacing black mask, with the glittering eyes staring at her, she could hardly believe she had spoken so boldly. She winced, waiting for a blow or a shot, but heard only silence.

The highwayman remained frozen a moment, then leapt into action. "Untie the coachman and postilion," he said. "See if you can revive Miguel and get some of that wine into him. We have to get them some help, quickly."

Marianne was so overwrought, and the man spoke with such authority, that she obeyed without question. She assumed that by "some help" he meant a doctor. It was a relief to have someone else take charge. She untied Beeton and left him to struggle with Tom's bindings.

"Tom's been hit. Just a flesh wound, it looks like," Beeton said. As Tom looked quite pleased with his wound, she decided it was not serious and continued following her orders.

While she poured wine down Miguel's throat, she was dimly aware of the men moving about, with the captain giving orders. They were lifting the duchess gently into the carriage, while the captain arranged her pillow and the blanket she carried against the autumn cold.

After a moment, the captain appeared at Marianne's side. "How is he?" he asked, taking Miguel's hand gently. Miguel had pulled down his mask. She noticed the grim set of the captain's jaw as he bent over his henchman, a small, dissipated-looking man with a scar running from the outer corner of his left eye to his jawbone.

"He's taken a little wine," she said.

Miguel opened his eyes and essayed an impish grin. "Wounded, not conquered," he said. "'Tis only a scratch on my arm, Cap'n. We've survived worse."

Marianne saw the blood on his sleeve and realized, though an arm wound was not life threatening, what a perilous business this robbing of travelers was. "How is the duchess?" she asked.

"Not dead," the captain replied. "Go to her. Keep her warm, and try to get some of that wine into her. I'll have a word with your coachman. There's a place nearby where we can get help."

This area was completely unknown to Marianne. She knew they were headed to London via Chertsey, and that is all she knew, for she had never been this far east. There wasn't a town or inn or even a house in sight. The highwaymen had chosen an isolated stretch of road for their attack. She had no recourse but to put the duchess's life, and her own, in the hands of this criminal and be grateful he didn't abandon them. She took the wine bottle and got into the carriage, where she propped the duchess up against a corner of the banquette and sat beside her. She arranged the blankets around her. It proved impossible to get her to drink.

In a moment, the carriage door opened. The captain and Miguel entered and sat on the banquette across from her. "You're not coming with us!" she cried. It was half a question, half a command. She hardly knew which of them was more frightening, the big man in the black mask or the little one with that disfiguring scar down his cheek.

"My friend is unable to ride," the captain replied. "Be careful how you breathe, Miguel. We would not want to contaminate the ladies," he said ironically. He handed Miguel a pistol — Beeton's antiquated gun, in fact — murmured a few words in some foreign language, and left. Were they Frenchmen? Her French was not good, but she usually recognized the language. It didn't sound like French. She had thought they were at least English criminals. English highwaymen had a reputation for their gentlemanly manners, so long as one went along with them. French highwaymen, on the other hand, were notoriously vicious.

This night, which had been miserable to begin with, became worse with every new development. As if being held up by highwaymen and the duchess being near death were not enough, she now had to share the carriage with this criminal. To add to the horror of it, the carriage soon left the public road, where they might meet someone who could help them, and entered a narrow, dark, rough path. The pallid daylight had vanished, plunging them into total darkness. They were in a tree-lined lane. She could hear the branches brush against the carriage.

"Where are we going?" she asked in alarm. "This can't be the road to a hospital."

"The captain knows where we're going," Miguel replied. "He's driving."

"Where is the coachman?"

"Him and t'other lad are riding our nags — and they'd best not cripple them. The captain is mighty fond of Juno."

She soon came to the conclusion that the captain was driving them to his lair, to conceal that he had killed the duchess, who had not stirred a muscle since her attack. He would not leave Marianne and the servants alive to bear witness. He was going to kill them all. That is why he was taking them down this narrow, twisty lane.

Why were Beeton and Tom going along with it? But with the duchess and herself as hostages, what choice did they have? The captain had taken their pistols from them. She was trapped for the present. She could not jump out and leave the duchess to these killers, but as soon as they reached their destination, she would try to work out some plan with Beeton.

The three of them should be able to overpower one man. Miguel was not able to fight with his wounded arm, though he could probably fire a gun well enough with his good one. She needed a weapon. She sat silent, mentally reviewing what was in the carriage. Blankets, books, reticules, a basket of apples, wine bottle. The bottle was the only item with any potential for inflicting damage. She would conceal it in her skirt and wait for an opportunity to strike the captain over the head with it as hard as she could and count on Beeton and Tom to overpower Miguel. It was not much of a plan, but it was the best she could think of over the next half hour while the carriage jiggled and jostled over the rough track.

After what seemed an eternity, Miguel stuck his head out the window and announced, "Nearly there, miss. It won't be long now."

The words no sooner left his mouth than there was a loud crack. Marianne's first thought was that the captain had shot Beeton. Before she could fly into a panic, the carriage lurched perilously and tilted. The left side hit the ground with a jerk. Marianne was kept busy preventing the duchess from sliding to the floor.

"The axle's gone," Miguel announced. "I'd best see if the cap'n needs a hand. No tricks now, miss." He waved the gun at her as he opened the door and leapt out.

Within seconds, he was joined by the captain. Marianne listened at the open window, but again they spoke that foreign language. She didn't understand a word they said, but she knew from their voices they were distressed. It did not seem the optimum moment to use her wine bottle, when Beeton and Tom were some yards away.

After a moment, the captain's head appeared at the window. "The cottage is only a few hundred yards farther. I'll carry the duchess. You follow me. Bring your bandboxes and anything you need."

When he opened the door, Marianne saw that he had removed his mask. It was dark in the carriage, however, and she could not really see what he looked like. He opened the door, bundled the duchess into the blanket, and lifted her into his arms. She was old and frail and the captain was young and strong. He carried her as lightly as if she were a sack of feathers. Marianne gathered up her reticule and the duchess's, added their bandboxes and the wine bottle, and followed him down a rutted lane to a cottage nestled in a clearing in what she now realized was a forest or spinney. The wind had risen. It bucketed the treetops and howled around her head, lifted her skirts and whipped the duchess's blanket about. A fine mist was in the air, not quite rain, but promising a deluge soon.

She took some comfort in seeing Beeton and Tom following on horseback. At least she would not be alone with these dangerous criminals. If it were not for the duchess, she would leap on that big bay mare with Beeton, and the three of them could thunder off to safety. But of course they could not abandon Her Grace.

The door of the cottage opened as they approached. A small, grizzled man in shirtsleeves welcomed them.

"Captain Jack! What brings you out on such a night?"

"Necessity, my friend. I have a sick lady here. Is there somewhere I can leave her?"

The man stood aside to let the captain enter. "You didn't shoot her, lad! The law takes a dim view of shooting your victims. There's no bribing your way out of murder."

Any hope that this man might help them died with this warning. He was a friend of the highwaymen.

"I said sick, not wounded," the highwayman replied. "Heart, I think, from the looks of her."

"This way." Their host took up a lamp and led them, with the captain carrying the duchess, through a cozy parlor to a small bedchamber at the back of the cottage. There was only the one story to the building and, she suspected, one bedchamber. Their host handed Marianne the lamp and left. She saw the room was modest, with a simple uncanopied bed, a chair, a toilet table, and a braided rug on the floor. A small fire was burning in the grate. She placed the lamp on the bedside table.

The room was at least clean. Marianne turned down the quilt to allow the captain to place the duchess on the bed.

"We have to send for a doctor," she said. She sensed that the duchess was looking a little better. Her complexion had a hint of color now.

"Ned, our host, is as good as a sawbones," the captain replied. He went to the duchess and felt her pulse, laid his hand along her cheek, and seemed satisfied.

"He is only a woodchopper or some such thing," Marianne objected. "You must get a proper doctor. Tell the man it is for the duchess. He'll come. We'll pay whatever he asks."

The highwayman lifted a well-arched eyebrow and said, "What will she use for money? Or is it your own two guineas you mean to spend?"

"I believe you will find the Duchess of Bixley's credit is good," she replied loftily.

The man's lips quirked in an amused way that was not quite a smile. In the confusion of settling the duchess, Marianne had not taken time to look at him closely. She stared at him now, assessing him as an opponent. He had a rugged, weathered face with a strong jaw. When he lifted his hand and removed his hat, she saw that his hair was as black as a crow's wing, with the same glossy iridescence. He wore it barbered close to his head, combed back, not brushed forward in the more stylish Brutus do. This surprised her, as his clothing was that of a dandy.

He was still in afternoon dress, but beneath his dark cape she glimpsed an elegant blue worsted jacket and a finely striped waistcoat of dark blue and yellow. A dotted Belcher kerchief was knotted casually at his throat in lieu of a white cravat. A pair of buckskins revealed a board-flat stomach and well-muscled legs. His top boots were a little the worse for dust, but they were of finest leather, not down at the heels. He wore no jewelry except a watch chain, with presumably a watch in his pocket. A ring could prove dangerous for a highwayman. One of his victims might recognize it if she saw him again and identify him by it.

His general appearance told her the captain was well-to-do, which only proved that he was a successful thief. She was more interested in assessing his character. That he was a thief already told her a good deal, but what sort of thief was he? Were there some personal weaknesses she might put to advantage? This would reveal itself in his eyes and mouth, and of course in his behavior. She studied his eyes. Dark blue, intelligent, heavily fringed — and pitiless. Her gaze lowered to his lips, which were set in a grim line. She could expect no mercy from this criminal. He would have abandoned her on the road with her dying mistress were it not for the severe penalty her death would bring him.

The penalty for a convicted highwayman was hanging, but it was commonly said that he could buy his way off the gallows for five hundred pounds as long as he had not physically harmed his victims. That was all their fine manners amounted to.

"Well, are you going to send for a doctor?" she asked.

"Let us ask the duchess if she wants one, if she is through with her performance now," he said, and turned toward the bed.

On cue, the duchess emitted a low moan, then opened her eyes and struggled up, resting against the pillows. "A sawbones will not be necessary, Marianne, but I shall have some of that wine now. Or brandy, if you have it, Captain."

"It will be my pleasure," the captain replied and left.

"Your Grace!" Marianne exclaimed in astonishment.

"I am fine now," the duchess said, "though I really feared I was going to have one of my attacks."

"But why did you —"

"I could not let that jackanapes ride off with my diamonds. I needed a ruse to stay with him. He has them in his pocket. He is a wide-awake scoundrel. He'll not be easy to fool. We must come up with a plan, or at least discover what cave or shack he calls home. He will not sell them to a fence right away. He knows I shall report the theft as soon as we reach civilization. The necklace will be too hot to unload for a month or two. Hush! He is coming back. We'll lay our plan later."

The tread of the highwayman's footfalls sounded like a death knell to Marianne.

CHAPTER
THREE

When the captain returned, the duchess lolled back against the pillows as if too weak to sit up. He was carrying a tray holding her brandy, along with a bottle of wine and one glass. Marianne assumed the wine was for himself, and was surprised when he passed the glass to her.

She felt in need of liquid courage and accepted it with an automatic, "Thank you."

"You are welcome, Miss Harkness," he replied punctiliously. "Shall I send Ned in to see you?" he asked Her Grace.

The duchess gave him a sneering look. "What is he, a horse doctor?" she asked.

"Yes, a very good one. He cured my Juno of the heaves," the captain said blandly.

She emitted a cackle of appreciation. "You are a cheeky rogue for one in your position. I shall not require your horse doctor's assistance. I am feeling stouter now."

"It is yourself who is in a vulnerable position, Your Grace," he pointed out. His tone was perfectly polite, but the firm timbre of his voice left no doubt who was in charge of the situation.

"Your high friends will be no help to you here," he continued, "and I fear I must detain you for the present. I shall undertake to see no harm comes to you so long as you do not leave the house. You may stay here a day or two until your carriage is repaired and you are well enough to continue on your way. If you are hungry, Ned can rustle you up some gammon and eggs. And now, if there is nothing else you require, I must leave."

"What about my companion and my servants?"

"They will be Ned's guests as well."

"Where is Miss Harkness to sleep? What assurance do I have that you will not be slipping into her room? A pretty young girl will be a strong temptation to you. She is under my protection."

The captain gave Marianne a brief, dismissing glance that displayed not an iota of interest in her charms. She might have been an old shoe or a bone. "I assure you I am no menace to your charge's virtue. She will have to sleep here with you in any case. The cottage has only the one bedchamber."

Marianne felt thoroughly embarrassed by both the question and his quick, dismissing answer. The captain bowed to them and left. The duchess took a sip of her brandy and said pensively, "He is well spoken for a common criminal, is he not?"

"He makes my flesh crawl."

"What you felt was a quiver of anticipation, Marianne, a shiver of romantic interest," she said with a naughty twinkle in her rheumy old eyes. "Naturally a well-bred young lady would not recognize it for that.

The man reeks of animal magnetism. Those low, mongrel types often do. I once had a chair man — But that is of no account now. You must be on your guard against his low-born charms, especially when he has drunk too much. These fellows all have a taste for hard liquor, loose women, and gambling, and a distaste for work. I mention it, as you will be seeing something of the fellow."

"No more than I can help."

"Don't be a Bath miss, Marianne. If I were half a century younger, I would do it myself. As I am old, I must count on your wiles to discover where he has hidden my diamonds." Marianne stared in belief. It was the first time she had ever been accused of possessing wiles. As to using them against this formidable captain, she would as lief try to ride a tiger.

The duchess continued unconcernedly, "The diamonds are not in his pocket. I gave it a jiggle as he handed me this brandy. They are still somewhere in this little cottage."

"He said he is going out. He'll take them with him."

"I think not. It is still the shank of the night. He is off to rob someone else. He would hardly take them with him, in case he is apprehended. No, he has certainly concealed them here in the cottage, and we must discover where. If you feel your charms are not up to the task of sweet-talking the captain, you will have to search the place after everyone has gone to sleep. It is true he displayed not one iota of interest in you."

"It is too dangerous, Your Grace! There will still be two men here. Miguel won't go out again. He has wounded his arm. He might kill me."

"Rubbish. They have had ample opportunity to kill us all if they wished. They would not dare to kill me or any of my employees. I have no patience with these missish quibbles. One would think *you* were the old invalid. You will feel better after you have finished your wine and eaten a bite. I am feeling peckish myself. Tell the horse doctor the old gray mare is ready for her oats now. Keep your eyes and ears open and see what you can discover while you are about it."

The duchess settled in as comfortably as if she were in her own mansion or a fine hotel. And it was not costing her a penny.

When Marianne went to the parlor, she saw the captain was at the door, just leaving. He stopped and leveled a scowl at her from those dark, dangerous eyes. He was not wearing his mask, but he was carrying it in his hand. His expression was wary, watchful. She felt as if he were looking right through her. She could no more sweet-talk this man than she could trade quips with an archbishop.

"Is there some trouble, Miss Harkness?" he asked. "Has Her Grace taken a turn for the worse?"

"No, she is fine," she said in a breathless voice.

"What is her trouble, exactly?"

"It is her heart. She had an attack a year ago. It bothers her still, especially when she is upset."

"You know how to deal with her problem?"

"I can handle it, as long as it is not a serious attack. I would feel better if she could see a doctor."

"If you run into trouble, call Ned. He has considerable experience with more than horses. If she is not unwell, why have you left her?"

"She is hungry."

"Ah, just so. You will find Ned in the kitchen," he said. He tipped his hat and turned to leave. Before stepping out, he stopped and turned back. His face had assumed a sneer. "By the by, your groom is fine. Tom's wound was not serious. Ned patched him up. No doubt you are concerned about him, though you did not bother to inquire." Then he left without molesting her.

Marianne drew a deep sigh of relief, both for Tom's safety and the highwayman's departure. In her nervous state, she had been too upset to think of the grooms. She wanted only to get away from the captain as quickly as possible.

She found her way to the kitchen with no difficulty. Ned was there, already busy at the stove. He looked up and smiled reassuringly. "Hungry, miss?" he asked.

Some sense of normalcy returned as she watched this ordinary-looking man stirring a pan of eggs in an ordinary kitchen, with a deal table and four chairs on one side, a blazing grate on the other, and the stove at the far end. The tension began to seep out of her stiff joints.

"Yes, I am. We didn't stop for dinner this evening," she replied. "Her Grace would like something as well, if it is not too much trouble."

"No trouble, miss. Captain Jack pays us well. Sit you down by the fire whilst I rustle up a bite."

The name Jack didn't suit him. He should have some more dangerous name, like Genghis Khan or Napoleon. She went to the grate but did not sit down. "Was Captain Jack in the army?" she asked, wondering why he was called captain. It occurred to her that he did have a military bearing and an officer's easy way with a command.

Ned laughed and began cracking more eggs into the pan. "Oh no, miss. It's what you might call an honorary title. Many of the scamps called themselves captain in olden times."

"He walks like a soldier," she said, hoping to learn more about the man. "An officer, I mean."

"He's no officer, but he is, or was, a gentleman, to judge by his ways. I don't ask questions. It might be best if you don't either, miss. The captain's very shy about his past," he said.

Ned began slicing bread. As he was busy, and as Marianne was accustomed to making herself useful, she offered to help him. He suggested she toast the bread at the grate with the long-handled fork kept there for the purpose. Ned busied himself with gammon and tea and setting up the tray. As they worked, they chatted.

"Are you a woodcutter by trade, Ned?" she asked.

"That I am, miss. I work for His Lordship. That's Lord Kerrigan. He owns this tract of land and several others hereabouts. I clear away the dead lumber for him and take down the trees he tells me to."

"The captain says you are a horse doctor as well."

"That is the captain's little joke, like. I know something about horses. I used to work at a breeding stable, but I was let go. His lordship wanted his nag to win a certain match. He gave me a bottle of medicine to give the horse before the race. The Jockey Club found out about it. One of us had to take the blame. For payment, his lordship lets me live here and look after this bit of forest."

"But that's horrid!"

"'Tis the way of the world, miss. The high and mighty look after themselves and let the devil take the hindmost." He handed her a tray holding the plates of gammon and eggs and tea. "There's a nice bit of supper for the old malkin and another for yourself. Sleep tight."

"Thank you, Ned."

She took the tray and returned to the duchess to relate what she had learned.

"The captain was leaving, you say? Where was he going?"

"I don't know."

"You should have found out. He must live hereabouts."

"They would never tell us, Your Grace. Ned warned me about asking questions. The only name I heard was from Ned. It is a Lord Kerrigan who owns this forest."

"I know the man. He is a scoundrel. Did the captain have my diamonds on him?"

"I don't know — but he was carrying his mask."

27

"Ah, then he is out attacking another innocent traveler, as I thought. Excellent. My diamonds are safe here."

The duchess had a hundred questions and complaints as she ate her supper. She wanted to know how Beeton and Tom were faring, how her horses were doing, who was going to repair her carriage, where was the closest constable's office, and why wasn't the tea hot.

When she had tired herself out, she handed Marianne one of the four pillows on her bed and told her to find herself a blanket and curl up by the grate.

Marianne did as she was told. It was preferable to sharing a bed with the termagant. She did not bother to undress, nor did she fall asleep easily. The duchess's stertorous snores shook the timbers. She lay awake for some hours, reliving the strange, horrible evening just past. She knew her mistress well enough to know she would not leave without her diamonds. And she had a sinking feeling that Captain Jack was not about to give them up. What would happen? What would become of her, of them all?

At length, she dozed off. When she awoke, the fire in the grate had died to a few glowing embers. The room was cold, but that was not what had awakened her. She had heard something, some sound within the cottage. The duchess? No, her snoring had subsided to a gentle rumble. The noise came again. Not in the cottage, but from outside. A horse — and presumably a rider. Had the captain returned? Who else could it be at this hour?

She sat up, every sense alive and alert, and went to open the bedroom door. In the darkness beyond, she heard the back door of the cottage open and stealthy footsteps enter. Someone went to meet the captain. She listened, but the sounds had ceased. The men were in the kitchen, talking. If she could get up and listen at the door, she might discover where the diamonds were hidden. She could steal them after the men went to sleep. She, the duchess, and the grooms could slip quietly away on foot and report these thieves to the closest constable. Beeton and Tom, she assumed, were sleeping in the stable.

She might not get another chance. The five years she had spent with the duchess had beaten much of the self-confidence out of her, but she had not always been so diffident. As she considered their predicament, she felt the old energy come to life again. She would do it! As a precaution, she went to the bed and jostled the duchess's arm. When the old lady grumbled awake, Marianne told her what had happened, and what she was going to do. She wanted someone to know and go to her rescue if she did not return. Or perhaps she wanted the duchess to forbid it.

"Excellent!" she crowed. "Go now, quickly, before Jack leaves with my diamonds. I am surprised you have it in you, Marianne, for you are usually such a sniveling, missish sort of gel. There is hope for you yet."

On these encouraging words, Marianne crept out of the room, into the pitch blackness beyond.

CHAPTER
FOUR

Across the room, slivers of yellow light shimmered in the darkness, showing her the location of the kitchen door. She crept toward it, feeling her way to prevent bumping into furniture in the unfamiliar parlor. The floor gave two light squawks. She froze, waiting for the kitchen door to fly open, shots to echo around her. There was no chair or sofa close enough to hide behind. After a moment, she realized they hadn't heard the sound, and she continued toward the door.

It was closed, but through it she could hear two masculine voices speaking in low tones. By pressing her ear to the panel, she could overhear their words. That arrogant buzz was Captain Jack, certainly. The other, however, did not sound like Ned. Was it Miguel? Yes, he had that touch of Irish brogue. Odd name for an Irishman, Miguel.

"You shouldn't have gone alone," he said. "I could have ridden, Cap'n. Sure 'tis only a scratch on my arm."

"Never mind, Mickey. I got him. I got the bastard." The captain's voice was gloating, thick with triumph. "I got him" sounded as if he had killed someone. A trickle of ice formed in Marianne's veins. What sort of monster was so delighted at having killed a fellow man? She took note of that "Mickey" as well. He *was* Irish, then. Miguel was his nom de guerre, as the other one's was Captain.

"How much?" Miguel asked.

"I haven't counted it." She heard the clink of coins.

"Gorblimey! It's thousands. How the devil did you carry it?"

"I can carry a heavy load, when it's gold," the captain said, and laughed a bold, triumphant laugh.

"Wasn't he riding with guards?"

"Three of them. I used my lasso, as we did to steal a steer in the old days."

"You didn't kill him?"

"Oh, no. I didn't touch a hair on his head." Marianne listened, frowning. "Got him" was a strange way to refer to robbing someone. Perhaps the captain had said, "I caught him." The door blurred some of their words.

"Nor his guards?"

"Why would I hurt his hirelings? I daresay they dislike him as much as I do. In any case they didn't try very hard to protect him."

"Well, you've done what you came to do. We can leave now. We'd best do it. He'll report it to the law."

"We'll lie low here for the nonce. The patrols will be out looking for us."

"Where will you hide it, in case they come looking?"

Marianne stiffened to attention and applied her ear more firmly to the door.

"In the usual place," he replied unhelpfully.

"Along with the diamonds?"

"Why not?"

"I'd put them in different places, then if they find one lot, they might not find t'other."

"Good thinking. I'll take care of it. I've earned a bottle of the best, don't you think?"

"That you have, Cap'n. You're a caution for sure. What your mama would say if she ever knew —"

"That is why she must never find out, Mickey. Not likely she will, as she seldom leaves home."

"She reads the journals, I suppose?"

The captain laughed. "It was Mama who taught me not to believe everything I read in the journals."

"I wager you believe in the results of the races at least. Have you read how my nag fared?"

There was the sound of bottles and glasses tinkling. It sounded as if they were settling in for a drinking bout. When the conversation turned to horses, Marianne thought it wise to leave, before they became drunk. She crept back to the bedroom, put a chair under the doorknob, and went to report to the duchess. The old lady was sound asleep. Some help she would have been in an emergency!

Marianne gave up any thought of sleep. She built up the fire and sat, scheming. The diamonds were here, somewhere in or near this little cottage. Where would the captain hide them? Not in the stable, with the grooms sleeping there. Not in the kitchen or parlor, where the ladies might be expected to venture. There were no other bedchambers. He had not ordered them to stay in their rooms, only inside the cottage. This suggested he had hidden the diamonds outside the cottage. Was there another building nearby?

Having arrived in the dark, she had little idea what places of concealment the environs might offer, but tomorrow she would find out. If he forbade her to go outside, she would spend time at every window until she discovered his hiding place, and slip out of bed the next night to recover the diamonds. Who else had he robbed tonight? He obviously knew the man would be passing by and carrying a supply of gold. How did he know that? Who was he? His mama appeared to be a respectable, educated woman, to judge by the conversation she had overheard.

As she closed her eyes, she heard the first chirp of birds outside the window. Although it was not yet daylight, the darkness was beginning to lighten.

When she awoke a few hours later, she had the strange sensation that she had slept for twenty hours. It was darker than when she had gone to sleep. She heard the patter of rain on the window, and when she looked out, she saw the sky was a dark, sullen gray that looked as if it would rain for forty days and nights, as in biblical times. Impossible weather for traveling, and difficult to make any excuse to go beyond the cottage to look for the diamonds. The bedroom window looked out on the spinney. If he had hidden the diamonds there, it would be like looking for a needle in a haystack.

The duchess soon stirred. She peered toward the grate and said in a querulous voice, "So, you got back. Where are my diamonds?"

Marianne gave a brief recital of her nocturnal spying adventure.

"Hmm. Outside, you think. I daresay you are right. Build up the fire, Marianne, and help me with my toilette. And order breakfast. Two soft-boiled eggs, not fried in that disgusting bacon fat as they were last night."

As the room was chilly, Marianne tended to the fire first, then tidied herself and went for water and to order breakfast. She found Ned alone in the kitchen. The fire was lit, water boiled on the hob, the aroma of coffee and bacon hung in the air. She asked for boiled eggs for the duchess, and he began to prepare them.

"How did you sleep, miss?" he asked.

"Fine. And you?"

"Like a baby. A terrible day," he said, glancing at the window.

"Yes, the roads will be a shambles."

"Mud to the axles. You're as well off here for the nonce."

"How soon do you think he'll let us go, Ned?"

"As soon as the roads are passable. It's no pleasure to him, having unwanted company, miss. He'll not stop you, once the weather clears."

She went to the window and stared out, looking all around at the stables, a kitchen garden well past its prime but with still some late vegetables growing, and, beyond, a small apple orchard. Unless the captain had buried his ill-got gains or hidden them in a tree, she did not think they were in that area.

When the tray was ready, she took it to the duchess and they ate their breakfast together, discussing their plight. Her Grace's chief interest was in recovering her diamonds. Marianne was concerned with making sure the grooms were alive and well. Quite apart from her feelings for them — and she liked the servants — if anything happened to them, she and the duchess would be at the captain's mercy. When they were finished, Marianne returned the tray to the kitchen.

"The duchess is concerned about her servants, Ned," she said. "Especially as Tom was wounded. Could I see them, just have a word with them to make sure they are all right?"

"I'll ask the captain when he wakes up, miss."

"Where is he sleeping?"

"In the stable. I slept on two chairs and a bolster by the hearth."

"I'm sorry. I expect we took your bedchamber."

"'Tis no problem, miss."

"The captain sleeps late," she said, glancing at the clock on the mantle. It was nine o'clock.

As she spoke, the back door opened and the captain entered.

CHAPTER
FIVE

Captain Jack wore the signs of his night's dissipation. His eyes, red from drink, and the whiskers shadowing his lower face, lent him an even more menacing air than before. His shirt was wrinkled and his jacket was dusty.

He clamped his lips in an angry line at seeing her in the kitchen, catching him in this unusual disarray. The captain was a little vain of his appearance.

"Is the duchess hungry again?" he asked ironically.

Impatience was beginning to wear Marianne's nerves thin. It was bad enough to have to take ridiculous orders from the duchess, but to have to grovel to a drunken criminal was the last straw.

"Yes, she has adopted the unaccountable habit of eating three times a day," she replied, and was astonished at her own bravery. She expected a sharp retort and a command to return to her room. To her astonishment, the captain looked a little sheepish.

"I daresay Ned can manage something?" he said, looking to Ned.

"The ladies have already ate, Captain. Missie was kind enough to bring back the tray."

"We do not expect you to perform such duties, Miss Harkness," the captain said. "Next time, just put the tray outside the door. It will be picked up."

She sensed a softening in his attitude and determined to make gain of it. "Why, to tell the truth, I am bored to flinders sitting by the grate all day. I would be happy to help Ned about the place. I shall clean up the kitchen for you, Ned."

"Certainly not!" the captain said at once, in his old, overbearing way.

"The young lady is worried about the servants, Captain," Ned said. "She'd like a word with them. I told her I'd ask you."

"They're fine," Jack said at once. "Beeton is busy repairing that broken axle. Best not to disturb him if you hope to get away today, Miss Harkness."

"I doubt anyone will be traveling today," Ned said, glancing out the window.

Jack frowned at the rain, which came coursing down the windowpanes in sheets. Occasional rumbles of thunder echoed beyond the window.

"I could go out to the stable," Marianne suggested. "That would not interfere with Beeton's work."

"It's pouring rain. You'd be drenched," Jack objected. "Ned has no umbrella."

Ned reached to a hook behind the door and tossed a blanket to her. "Here, put this over your head, miss. That's what I do. And mind the puddles."

"Thank you, Ned." Marianne snatched it up and darted out the door before the captain could order her to stay put. The path to the stable was cobblestoned and did not do much harm to her slippers. She found Beeton working on the axle, as the captain had said.

"How is Tom, Beeton?" she asked.

When Beeton looked up from his work, she saw his left eye was dark and swollen. "Beeton! What happened? You didn't have that bruise the last time I saw you. Did he beat you?"

"He's a fair fighter," Beeton allowed grudgingly. "We had a few rounds last night. When he came back from wherever he went, he caught me peeking in the windows of the cottage. I wanted to make sure you and Her Grace were safe. That's all, but the captain took the notion I was spying on him."

"He robbed another carriage. I overheard him and Miguel discussing it last night. They got away with thousands of pounds of gold. They had it right in the kitchen. Did you see where he put the gold?"

"Nay, but he left early this morning carrying a heavy bag. He rode off down the lane. No knowing which way he went. Two robberies in one night! He's ambitious then, isn't he? Before he left last night he told me and Tom not to leave the stable. He had a dog guarding the door, but I always had a way with dogs. He took the hound this morning. I'm thinking he thought I was looking for the diamonds. If we find that hound, we might find the sparklers, eh?"

"Yes, that's an idea. He was going to hide the diamonds and the gold separately."

"I've tried to get out, but Ned keeps a sharp eye from the kitchen. They have our guns. We're as good as prisoners here, miss. Are you and the old lady all right?"

"They haven't harmed us, but we must get away, Beeton. Where is Tom? How is his arm?"

"It's recovering. The captain dressed his wound and fixed him up with a bandage. Tom is giving Miguel a hand with the horses."

"The duchess insists she won't leave without her diamonds."

"Better to leave without them than not to leave at all. Tell her that. We could come back with a couple of Bow Street Runners to search the place."

"Do you think we could overpower them? Is Tom able to wield a stick?"

"He's not much of a scrapper at the best of times. If we could get hold of a pistol . . ."

"Yes, you're right. We need a gun. I'll try to get one. You said Ned has one in the kitchen. I daresay that is why the captain forbade me to help out there."

"Very likely."

"I shall insist. And if he won't let me, then I'll be there ten times a day, demanding hot water and food and tea and anything I can think of. Ned is bound to be off his guard sooner or later."

"The captain —" Beeton came to a sudden stop.

"Devil take the captain! Bad enough to be under the duchess's paw from dawn till dark, but to be ordered about by an upstart thief —"

As she spoke, she noticed Beeton was making strange faces, drawing his eyebrows, and frowning. She thought it was disapproval of her plans and wondered why he didn't speak. Then it occurred to her that someone was listening. She turned around and saw Captain Jack not a yard behind her, staring at her with those dark eyes and a disparaging grin on his face. He had not bothered with a blanket. Raindrops speckled his head and shoulders as he stood, arms akimbo, as if he owned the world and everything in it. Such arrogance from a highwayman made her blood boil.

"You may catch Ned off guard. But you will find the upstart thief eternally on the *qui vive*, Miss Harkness," he said. "You have seen your coachman is well. You may return to the house now."

She turned on him in a fury that was half embarrassment. "Beeton is *not* well! You have beaten him. As an experienced highwayman, I trust you know the law is harsh on those felons who abuse their victims, Captain."

"Only if the felon is caught, miss," he said. "I have no intention of being caught, by you or anyone else. Carry on, Beeton."

He clamped his fingers on her elbow and led her back to the house at such a brisk gait she could hardly keep up with him. He stopped at the back door before entering and turned to face her, still holding on to her arm.

"You are not to leave the house again," he said. He spoke grimly, with a menacing frown.

She noticed, then, that he had shaved, combed his hair, brushed his jacket, and put on a fresh shirt and cravat. Why had he taken the time, when he was obviously concerned about what she was doing in the

40

stable? He had a wide streak of the dandy — yet who was there to impress in this godforsaken place except herself?

She was no beauty, but she was at least a lady and companion to a duchess. That might impress a common criminal. The man gave himself airs, but a true gentleman would never behave as he behaved. Would it be possible to sweet-talk him into returning the diamonds, as the duchess had suggested? It was worth a try at least.

She gave a long sigh. "It is so boring, sitting all day with Her Grace, with nothing to do," she said, casting a sulky look at him.

The glitter in his eyes lightened to a sparkle, not far removed from a twinkle. His grim lips softened slightly. "Perhaps we could arrange a game of cards this afternoon to lighten the tedium," he suggested.

She allowed her eyelashes to flutter. "Oh, could you, Captain? That would be lovely."

"Shall we make it a date, Miss Harkness?" He was definitely smiling now. "But I give you fair warning, I seldom lose — at cards."

This was said not in a menacing way but almost with an air of flirtation. She replied in the same vein, flicking her eyes over his face and smiling, as she had seen the flirts at the assembly rooms in Bath do, on those rare occasions when she was invited to join Her Grace.

"Are you sure your name is Captain Jack? You sound more like Captain Sharp. There is an old saying, lucky at cards, unlucky in love. I have never been lucky in love, but I wager you have known success with the ladies. I look forward to the game."

The last vestige of severity melted at her coquettish speech. His lips opened in a slow, devastating smile that softened the harshness of his saturnine face as he gazed down at her until she felt a warmth suffuse her cheeks. She watched his transformation, bewitched, and did not realize at once that his smile was more dangerous than his wrath. The shiver that scuttled down her spine reminded her of the duchess's warning of his magnetism.

He opened the door and held it while she went in. He helped her remove the blanket and hung it on the hook. As he performed these courtly gestures, she tried to marshal her thoughts.

She turned to him, still smiling. "The duchess wants some hot water, but you need not wait for me, Captain. Ned will get it for me. I'm sure a busy man like you has more important things to do."

"Not at all. We thieves seldom rob a coach in broad daylight — especially in such a deluge. So hard on the toilette. I shall take the water to Her Grace for you, Miss Harkness. I, too, find the days long and tedious."

She didn't bother arguing. The captain was not flirting now. That edge of steel was back in his voice and his eyes. He had seen right through her and was annoyed with her charade. He would not be an easy man to con. But she felt she had gained an insight into her captor. He was vain; he liked women; he enjoyed flattery, even if he didn't believe it. She had driven a small wedge into his iron armor and would see if she could pry it open further that afternoon.

CHAPTER
SIX

Marianne reported to the duchess that Tom was fine and Beeton was repairing the carriage. She did not mention her attempt at flirtation with the captain. The old lady's sharp tongue would only make her feel a fool.

"Beeton thinks we should leave as soon as possible and come back with a couple of Runners to look for the diamonds. They will not be much good to you if you are shot trying to recover them, ma'am."

"I don't recall asking for Beeton's opinion on how to run my life," was Her Grace's reply. "No one would dare to shoot me."

"The captain dared to give Beeton a black eye last night," Marianne said, making much of Beeton's loyalty and danger in trying to ascertain that his mistress was safe.

"He is well paid to look after me," she said. This did not mean that the duchess's cold heart was untouched. Her talk was harder than her heart, and Marianne knew it. "Is he badly hurt?" she asked a little later.

"Not so far. Bearing in mind that Ned is standing guard with a pistol and that Tom has been shot as well,

I do think it dangerous to remain here a moment longer than necessary, but of course the decision is up to you."

"So it is. I am glad you realize it."

There was a tap at the door. When Marianne went to answer it, the captain stepped in, carrying a jug of hot water for Her Grace.

"So, villain! You have been beating my servants!" was her greeting.

The captain's dark eyes turned to Marianne. A twist of contempt moved his lips, making her feel like a schoolgirl who had carried tales to the teacher.

"Your coachman and I amused ourselves with a bout of fisticuffs last night, Your Grace. No one was beaten. Miss Harkness will tell you how heavily time lies on one's hands in such weather as this."

"I do not need anyone to tell me! I am being confined against my will in a dirty hovel, ill fed, ill treated. That is kidnapping, sir. As a veteran criminal, you do not need to be told that is a hanging offence. Your body will hang from the gibbet at the crossroads for rats to gnaw on and crows to peck at. You'll not bribe your way out of this crime."

Marianne saw the indecision on the captain's face. She was surprised that the duchess's threat had such a good effect. She hadn't thought the man capable of fear.

"I brought you here because it was the closest place when you were ill. You are free to go at any time, Your Grace," he replied. "If you prefer trudging through mud to your waist, you can leave this minute."

"Naturally I cannot leave until my carriage is repaired. That ought not to have taken more than an hour. It is a ruse to keep me confined."

"Ned had to take an axle from another carriage. The carriage is repaired now. Shall I have it sent for?"

They all looked out the window, where the rain came down in sheets, obliterating vision. The spinney beyond was a smear of green in the distance.

"Do you take me for an idiot?" she asked. "Naturally we cannot leave until the rain lets up. The instant it stops, we shall leave. And I suggest you do likewise, sir, for it will not be long until the law is here looking for you."

"It is kind of you to give me fair warning, ma'am." He bowed and headed for the door As he passed Marianne he said in a perfectly civil tone, "You have not forgotten our date, Miss Harkness? Perhaps Her Grace would like to join us? The woodchopper, the duchess, the highwayman, and you — a delightful foursome for a few hands of whist, *n'est-ce pas*? If the rain obliges us by continuing, *c'est-à-dire*."

Before she could reply, he strode nonchalantly from the room.

As the door closed, the duchess pulled her shawl angrily about her and said, "I told him a thing or two."

"I am happy you have decided to leave as soon as possible," Marianne said.

She knew it was not the first time the duchess's temper had led her from her preferred course. She had no wish to leave until she recovered her diamonds, but having said she would, she might go through with it. Or

46

on the other hand, she might have another convenient heart attack. There was no saying with the duchess.

"What is this about playing cards, Marianne? I should not mind a few hands of whist. It would be better than sitting here, looking out at that miserable rain. And nothing to read in the house, of course."

"Perhaps the captain can't read," Marianne said.

"Not read? Don't be a fool. Of course he can read. He is well spoken — even a bit of French. He has rubbed shoulders with quality folks at some point in his life. A gentleman's valet, perhaps. He knows enough to call a duchess Her Grace at least. The more ignorant class call us Your Ladyship. He hasn't one of those lumpish, common faces, either. He is fine-boned. A by-blow of some gentleman, no doubt. What is his last name? Fitz-something, is it? Fitz-Matthew, I shouldn't wonder. He has something of the look of the Everetts. Old Matthew was a bit of a womanizer."

"I don't know his last name," Marianne replied.

"Making dates to play cards with total strangers? I shall ask him his name the next time he comes to call." Her proud neck gave a jerk when she realized what had slipped out. "That is, the next time I require his services. It is his speaking decent English that leads one astray and makes one forget he is not a gentleman. You want to be on guard against that, Marianne. Don't think because he wears a decent jacket and calls you Miss Harkness that he has the morals of a gentleman. He would take advantage of a simpleton like you in a minute if you gave him half a chance. I must certainly chaperon you at that card game this afternoon. I wager he is a regular Captain Sharp. I shall keep an eye out for marked cards. Pour the water for me. I shall have a wash now."

The morning passed in scolding and complaining and anticipation of catching the captain cheating at cards. When the duchess became tired of her bedchamber, she decided the chimney was smoking and moved out to the parlor. Marianne examined the grounds from the window but could spot no likely place of concealment for the diamonds. It was just unkempt grass with a few random trees and shrubs. She made half a dozen trips to the kitchen but had no opportunity to search for the gun. Ned was always there. After a few visits he became suspicious and watched her closely.

"We are hunting a mare's nest," the duchess decided. "We shall leave without the diamonds and send the police here to search for them. I wager the captain has spirited them away long since, along with that cache of gold. I have not seen hide nor hair of him for hours. Bow Street will find him and make him talk."

"I think we should leave as soon as possible," Marianne agreed.

Lunch created a little diversion. Ned had killed a chicken and roasted it. They dined on that and bread that was becoming stale. The duchess and Marianne ate alone at the table. Marianne wondered where the others ate, as there was only the one table in the house. She could not think the captain would be eager to keep them longer than necessary when they caused such a commotion. He must be eager to return to his own home, wherever it was. Probably some shack in the forest. But as she considered his clothes, she began to wonder how he turned out so elegantly without a valet. Try as she might, she could not envisage the captain polishing his own boots — nor Miguel, if he did double duty as valet, doing such a fine job on his cravats.

At three o'clock, the captain came in the front door, shaking rain from his curled beaver. They had not seen him since his morning visit to deliver the water to Her Grace. The duchess's spirits revived remarkably upon his entrance. She did not smile, but there was a noticeable glint in her eyes.

"Ready for our card game, ladies?" he asked.

The cards were a strong temptation to the old dame, but she stuck to her decision to leave. "We are ready to leave, sir," she said. "I see the rain has let up. There is hardly a drop on your shoulders."

"The rain is letting up, but the roads are wretched. I have been out checking them. Another day cannot make much difference."

"Not make much difference?" she said, outraged. "Do you think I have rattled all the way from Bath in my condition for no reason? If we do not get to London by Saturday, I shall miss my great-granddaughter's wedding, which I have come a hundred miles to see. I was planning to wear my diamond necklace," she added, giving him a black, accusing stare.

He looked at her blandly and asked, "Who is being married?"

"No one you would know, Captain. They are both members of the nobility."

"You are mistaken, ma'am. I frequently rob members of the nobility."

Amused at his brass and eager to boast of her connections, she said, "I shall satisfy your vulgar curiosity, if you wish. There can be no danger in it, as all the parties concerned are already safe in London. Lady Augusta Sinclair is to marry Lord Agnew, the eldest son of the Duke of Stornway."

When Captain Jack stared at her a moment in surprise, Marianne took the notion he did know them. Perhaps he had relieved Lady Augusta of her jewelry.

He said, "On Saturday, you say. That leaves you three days. You are only twenty miles from London. You can wait another day for the roads to settle."

The duchess drew back her ears like an angry mare and said, "Am I to understand you are forbidding us to leave, Captain?"

"Certainly not, madame. You are not a prisoner, after all."

She gave a *harrumph* of derision.

"I am merely advising you against it."

"Call my carriage, at once!" She rose and said to Marianne, "Come along, Marianne. Pack up my bandbox and let us prepare." She strode across the humble little parlor to the bedchamber with all the pride of a lioness traversing the plains of Africa.

The captain turned to Marianne. "Can you talk her out of this foolishness? The roads are inches deep in mud. She'll not get a mile. If she has to walk back, she might have another attack."

"She is intractable when she has made up her mind."

"You are eager to get away as well, I expect?"

"Yes, I am. I am not accustomed to living in a place like this." She looked around at the spartan little chamber.

"You are accustomed to doing your running and fetching in more elegant surroundings, no doubt," he sneered. "A touch of reality would do you both the world of good."

"We have already endured several hours of what you choose to call reality. I feel none the better for it, Captain."

"I was referring to your mistress, actually," he said, a touch of apology in his voice. "I can see your life is no bed of roses. I'll go along with you until you get across the bridge. If you make it that far, it is only a mile to Chertsey. We shall have to part company then, I fear, as she will be laying her charge against me at Chertsey."

"Yes," Marianne said, and found, to her astonishment, that she felt a little twinge of regret, pity, or some tender emotion. It was his concern for their safety that caused it. He was a highwayman, a criminal, but he had some good instincts. He seemed to have some genuine concern for their welfare at least.

They stood a moment, looking at each other uncertainly. "Well, it is goodbye then, Miss Harkness," he said in that hearty voice of one ill at ease but determined not to show it. He put out his hand to shake hers.

She automatically gave him her hand. He held it in his strong, warm fingers a moment longer than necessary.

"I am sorry we never had our card game," she said, withdrawing her fingers.

"I am sorry we had to meet under such inauspicious circumstances," he replied rather jerkily, as if he did not quite want to say it, or perhaps was just unaccustomed to being polite to ladies.

She didn't have to try to flirt him into anything now. They were leaving. They would not see him again, unless it was at Newgate. An image of the captain with a noose around his neck popped into her head.

She gazed at him with a sad, earnest expression and said, "I wish you would quit this dangerous life. Highwaymen seldom live more than a year or two, Captain."

"There are reasons why I do this, Miss Harkness," he replied. His tone was resolute, not sorry at all.

"Money is no reason to risk your life — and to rob innocent people," she added, almost as an afterthought.

"I don't rob innocent people."

"You robbed the duchess."

"Of one necklace. I wager she has dozens of them."

Marianne gave him a chiding look and turned to go. She turned back after a step and found him looking at her wistfully. She said, "What is your name, Captain? Your family name?"

"Macheath," he replied. The sober mood of their parting had dissipated. An echo of his rakish grin curved his lips, but his eyes shone softly, sending a warm glow through her.

"Goodbye, Captain Macheath."

Then she hurried into the bedchamber to pack the bandboxes. The duchess was arranging her bonnet.

"What kept you?" she asked in her usual irritable way.

"I asked the captain his name. It's Macheath. That is Scottish, is it not?"

"Macheath? Yes, and I am Polly Peachum. Idiot! He was bamming you. Captain Macheath is a famous fictional highwayman, from Gay's *Beggar's Opera*. Well, it was too much to expect he would give his real name. We shall learn it when he is arrested. Hurry up, child. We haven't got all day."

As Marianne folded up nightgowns and shawls, she felt cheated. She had thought, for a moment, that the captain might be capable of redemption, that he was not quite rotten to the core. And all the time he had been laughing up his sleeve at her. Captain Macheath, indeed!

"There, we are ready," she said, gathering up the odds and ends to straggle out to the carriage, balancing the second bandbox on top of the first, with a blanket trailing over her arm. The duchess carried nothing but her reticule and the heavy burden of her pride.

CHAPTER
SEVEN

The roads were every bit as bad as the captain had warned. The carriage wheels creaked at each turn as they lurched through inches of mud.

"It will be better once we are out of this track and back on the paved road," the duchess said, more to cheer herself than her companion.

Marianne scoured the surroundings for possible hiding places for the diamonds. As the forest grew right up to the verge of the lane, she could see little but trees. If there was a shed or shack in there it would be hard to find.

The captain rode in front of them on Juno, a handsome bay mare with a black mane and tail. He looked every inch the gentleman with his curled beaver tilted over his eyes and a well-cut jacket hugging his broad shoulders. Miguel, his arm in a sling, rode behind on a brown cob. The sky was a dull gray, the countryside sodden from the recent downpour. Branches, their leaves weighted with water, drooped mournfully. Between the dreary day, the wretched road, and the loss of the diamonds, it was hard to keep up one's spirits.

Marianne tried to be happy that they had escaped the highwayman and were on their way to the grandest wedding of the year. She was to attend. She had never met Lady Augusta nor her groom, but the duchess had arranged it as a treat for her and because she might require Marianne's services at the reception. Marianne knew to a nicety how the duchess liked her shawl and pillow arranged — she always traveled with a pillow in case her back went out. She was a martyr to her rheumatism and was surprised it was not paining her in such damp weather as this. It was handy, too, to have someone to carry the various medicinal decoctions and powders that accompanied her wherever she went.

"There, you see! I knew we would make it," the duchess cried as they drew out of the lane onto the main road. It had taken more than half an hour to traverse the mile of lane. Already the autumn sky was darkening. "It will be easy driving from here on. We shall spend the night at Chertsey and proceed to London tomorrow, and have two days to rest up for the wedding. I shall arrange for someone to give you a little tour of London, Marianne. It is shocking for a young lady never to have seen St. Paul's and the Tower of London. I don't know what you were about, never to have seen them. Very remiss of you."

It was the shops and such delights as the theater that Marianne would have preferred to see, but that was unlikely. Her escort would be some old friend of the duchess's. All her hopes of future happiness were pinned on meeting some respectable and undemanding gentleman at the wedding.

The road was by no means smooth, but it was better than the lane. Were it not for the grit that had invaded the hubs of the wheels and creaked at every turning of the axle, the drive would have been tolerable. They proceeded another few miles at a faster pace until they came to the river. What was usually no more than a meandering stream had swollen to a brown torrent after the recent deluge. The water rose to within an inch of the little wooden humpback bridge that would take them to the other side. The bridge was only ten yards wide, but it was a vital link in their journey.

Beeton drew the horses to a stop before crossing it. The duchess was just opening the window to holler up to him when the captain appeared at the window.

"I don't recommend you cross the bridge," he said. "I rode over it. The weight of my mount was enough to cause it to sway. The torrent must have loosened its moorings."

"Rubbish," the duchess said. With the lure of Chertsey on the other side — proffering a comfortable bed, a decent meal, and civilized company — she was not about to turn around. Where was there to go, but back to that woodchopper's shack? "Carry on, Beeton!" she called.

Beeton joined the captain. "That bridge must be a hundred years old, madam. It's trembling in the wind. Is there another bridge not too far away, Captain?"

"Two miles in the other direction. You'd have to turn the carriage around and go back —"

"We are not turning back!" the duchess declared. "Carry on, Beeton." She closed the window, and Beeton, with a shake of his head, returned to his perch.

"It is some trick to steal our nags," the duchess declared as the carriage lurched into motion. "No doubt Macheath has his henchmen waiting at the other bridge."

Marianne looked out the window behind them. The captain and Miguel watched them from the entrance to the bridge. When the captain raised his hat and waved farewell, she felt a sense of loss, like a hollowness inside, in spite of all the trouble he had caused. It had been interesting to be in company with a handsome young man, someone so different from the duchess's crones.

The horses balked at traversing the unsteady bridge. The bridge swayed, the carriage lurched, and both ladies hung on to the edge of the banquette with both hands. Marianne prayed. As the duchess's lips were moving silently, Marianne assumed she was ordering God to get them across safely. They were already halfway to the other side. The bridge was not sinking, was it? That creaking sound could not be the sound of timbers failing. It was only the suspension belts of the carriage. They would make it. Surely they would make it.

There was no warning crash of failing wood. The bridge did not break under the weight of the carriage and drop them into the water, but they were suddenly driving at an odd, steep angle that catapulted the duchess off her banquette and onto the floor. The carriage began to bounce and jerk. Marianne, sitting with her back to the horses, was pitched up with her head bumping the ceiling. The sound of horses neighing in panic was followed by a shout and a splash, and suddenly muddy water was seeping in around the edges of the carriage doors. The moorings on the far side of the bridge had washed loose, causing the bridge to form a wooden slide leading into the river.

The duchess, for once, was silent. It was Marianne who spoke. "Are you all right, Your Grace?" she cried in alarm as she scrabbled to the floor to assist her mistress, who was pale and scowling fiercely, but in no dire condition.

"Of course I am not all right! I am drowning."

The water was rushing in quickly, but it covered no more than their feet and the hems of their skirts. The carriage continued to jerk and sway as the horses flailed and the racing river raged.

"Beeton! I say, Beeton! Get me out of here before I drown. Damme, that water is cold as ice. Our trunks, Marianne! If they land in the river, I shan't have a stitch to wear to the wedding!"

Marianne looked out the window. "The water is not very deep," she said. "The horses are trying to scramble up the bank. They'll never make it. Oh dear, I hope they don't lame themselves!"

The duchess shoved Marianne aside and hollered out, "Beeton! Mind the horses!"

Beeton and Tom were in the water up to their waists, trying to help the team up the bank. But it was a sheer drop with no foothold.

"We are going to drown," the duchess said in a voice of doom. "Drown in a dirty river in the middle of nowhere. Can you swim?"

"No."

"Then crawl up on the roof of the carriage and shout as loud as you can until someone hears you. Go on, get out."

"I can't get the door open. The water is holding it shut."

"Can you squeeze out the window?"

"I'll try. But what about you —"

"We don't seem to be sinking any deeper. I'll wait here. What is Beeton about? Why doesn't he get us out?"

"He's trying to save the horses."

"Damn the horses. Tell him to save me."

Help came not from Beeton but from Captain Macheath. He had seen their predicament and ridden his mount into the swollen river to help them. He appeared at the window in water to his waist, wearing only his shirt and trousers. He handed his jacket to the duchess for safekeeping.

"Sit tight, ladies," he said. "I'll help Beeton unhitch the nags. The bank is less steep farther downstream. You won't drown in this shallow water. The carriage wheels are already resting on the riverbed. There's no danger of tipping. We'll come back and rescue you. Miguel is riding ahead to get help at the closest inn."

The duchess tossed the captain's jacket aside and reached out the window to clasp his hand in her bony, bejeweled fingers. "Hurry, Captain," she said.

His mount half swam, half walked on to the front of the carriage as he gentled it by soft urgings. He dismounted and began working with Beeton and Tom to rescue the team, with water churning all around them. Marianne put her head out the window to watch. Macheath's sodden shirt clung to him, revealing his body through the linen material, which had become transparent from the water. That darker part in front would be a patch of hair on his chest. The muscles of his shoulders and upper arms tensed to bulges as he strained to steady the horses. His broad back tapered to a slender waist. He had an athlete's body, strong yet agile and graceful, even under great physical exertion. She had never seen a man so close to naked, which she felt accounted for the unusual heat growing inside her.

When Macheath turned and glanced back at her, his little smile told her he liked the chance to show off in front of a lady. She quickly drew her head in.

The duchess immediately took her turn at the window. "A fine figure of a man," she said grudgingly. "It is the inbreeding that robs the nobility of a figure."

The carriage swayed a little, but the fear of death had passed, leaving Her Grace somewhat chastened.

"Fancy that," she said. "Rescued by a thief and a scoundrel. I knew there was some good blood in the lad. Did I not say his papa was a gentleman, Marianne?"

Marianne did not answer, but she wore a little smile of satisfaction. "Lift your feet up out of the water, Duchess. Here, let me wrap the blanket around them."

"I'll have a sip of that wine, Marianne, to restore my nerves. What a blessing I didn't have one of my attacks, or you would be lumbered with a corpse. It might happen yet. If it does, take my body home. I want to be buried at Bath. My lawyer has all the details."

"You have no intention of dying, and you know it," Marianne scolded.

The old girl was fairly docile during the interval while the men were rescuing the team. She did not allow Marianne another shot at the window. It was twenty minutes before Macheath returned to the carriage, at which time Her Grace pulled her head inside and pretended her interest had been for the horses. Macheath's complexion was even more highly colored than usual after his exertion. One shock of wet hair tumbled over his forehead, giving him a youthful air.

"We managed to save the team," he assured them. His navy eyes turned to Marianne and surveyed her closely, as if looking for signs of damage. When he ascertained that she was well, he addressed himself to the duchess. "One of the nags has a stretched tendon, but he'll recover. Beeton and Tom are taking them to the inn. They'll come back or send men back to rescue the carriage. Are you able to walk, duchess?"

"Of course I can walk. I am not a cripple, but I can't walk on water."

"That surprises me," he said blandly. "You'll have to scramble out the window, I fear. We won't get the door open against the pressure of the water. Can you make it?"

"If I must." She stuck her head out the window but seemed unable to get through.

Macheath peered in at Marianne. "You push her from behind, I'll pull. Ready?"

"Ready."

She put her hands around the duchess's bony hips and tried to push her out. With Macheath pulling at her shoulders, she was finally hauled out the window grumbling and complaining and threatening a heart attack and enjoying it all keenly. Macheath gathered her up in his arms and waded through the muddy river until they reached a spot where the slope of the bank was gentle enough to allow her to clamber up, with his help.

"It's chilly," he said. "Are you going to be all right?"

"My shawl is not quite drenched. Thank you, Captain."

"My pleasure, Duchess," he replied, and gave a gallant bow before darting back down to rescue Marianne. She was young and agile. By bracing her feet against the banquette, she got out the window with no trouble, carrying the captain's jacket, as she feared he'd catch his death of cold.

Macheath gathered her into his arms. She had never felt so uncomfortable in her life. It seemed shamefully intimate to be held against that hard, wet chest, with his arms around her and his chin brushing the top of her head.

"Put your arm around my neck," he suggested. "It'll help balance the load."

She shyly put one arm around his neck. "I hope I'm not too heavy," she said.

"Light as a feather."

"I weigh eight stone."

"It's well distributed," he murmured. She peered up at him, wondering if he referred to her arm around his neck. She saw the laughter in his eyes: "It would be running after your harpy mistress that keeps you in such good shape. Why do you do it?"

"Because I have no money."

"An orphan?"

"Yes."

"Shall I hold up a coach and steal a dowry for you?"

"No, thank you."

"Poor, but proud, eh?"

"Poor and honest, Captain Macheath. Which is not your name, by the by. You stole it from *The Beggar's Opera*."

"Borrowed it. You can hardly expect me to announce my real name. We upstart thieves always work under an alias."

She smiled shyly at him. "You may be a highwayman, but you are a gallant one, sir."

"Why thank you, ma'am. All in a day's work for us heroes."

As he spoke, he tripped over a rock on the river floor. He stumbled, tried to keep his balance, and failed. The hero and his cargo both landed in the water, gasping for breath. When Marianne struggled to her feet, the muddy torrent was up past her waist. The water was colder than she had imagined. She shivered as the brisk wind blew. Macheath's jacket, which she had been carrying, was dripping. Her bonnet was sodden. She pulled it off, decided it was beyond redemption, and consigned it to the river. Her wet hair hung in dripping tendrils around her face. She reached up and brushed the muddy water from her eyes with the back of her hand. Macheath shook his head, like a dog coming out of the water. His hat was already gone with the current. He took his jacket and tied it around his waist.

"My valet might be able to do something with it," he said.

"Your valet?"

"The inn has a fellow who valets for the guests. Sorry for your dunking, Miss Harkness. I tripped. That will teach me to attempt to do two things at once. Shall we try again?" He reached to gather her into his arms once more.

"I'm soaked now. I might as well walk," she said, and began walking along the river. The uneven bottom and the rushing water made her footing unsteady.

"It was an accident, you know," he said with an air of apology, walking along beside her.

When she stumbled, he reached out and took her hand. "Forgive me?"

"There is nothing to forgive. About falling in the water, I mean. As to the rest, it is unforgivable, and you know it, Captain."

"You're a hard woman, Marianne Harkness."

"And you, Mr Whoever-You-Are, are incorrigible."

"The right lady might be able to reform me," he said with a quizzing smile. "You forget my gallantry."

64

He tilted his head down at her. She peered up and could not control the answering smile that peeped out. He had practically saved her life, after all. Other than the duchess's losing her diamonds, the past hours had been rather fun. Well, exciting. This adventure would be something to remember when she was back at Bath, at the duchess's beck and call. Nothing like this was likely to happen to her again. She would never meet another man like Captain Macheath.

"Well, you are somewhat gallant," she allowed.

"There now, that didn't hurt a bit, did it?" he said, tightening his grip on her fingers.

CHAPTER
EIGHT

The highwayman continued to win favor with the ladies by rendering them every assistance possible in their distress. He knew of a simple cottage nearby where they could wait by the fire while he went to the closest inn to beg or borrow a carriage. He was soon back with a handsome rig and blankets. One glance at the setup told Marianne that neither the glossy black carriage nor the team of spanking bays was provided by the inn. Where had he got the rig, and on such short notice? "A charitable couple lent it when they heard of the duchess's distress," he said.

But that could not account for his change of clothes. He was wearing a dry jacket and buckskins and a clean shirt. He had even changed his top boots. The jacket fit perfectly — it was his own. He must live nearby.

He had taken the liberty of hiring rooms for them. He assumed they would like to bathe and change into dry clothes while the carriage was being dried and cleaned before proceeding to London. Beeton could attend to the horse's pulled tendon at the same time.

"As it is now quite dark, I thought you might like to stay overnight and continue to London tomorrow, Your

Grace. There is always a danger of highwaymen this close to London, you must know."

"Well, upon my word!" she gasped, overcome by the fellow's brass.

Marianne, too, started at this mischievous speech. She was sure the duchess would flare up at him, but after she recovered her breath, she actually laughed.

"He is too late. He would get slim pickings from me this night," she said. "What we ought to do, now that we have made it over the bridge, is continue on to Chertsey."

"True, but you would not like to land in on your hostess in such disarray. You must be still trembling from the accident as well."

"So I am. We shall remain overnight at the inn, Macheath. I hope they have aired the beds."

"I took the liberty of asking them to do so, ma'am. I have hired adjoining rooms for you, ladies. My gift, as you are a trifle short of funds at the moment."

His behavior was strangely ambiguous: offering every assistance on the one hand, while reminding them of past offenses on the other. Marianne could make nothing of it but was glad for his help.

The inn was a quaint, pretty place of ancient vintage with intricately patterned brickwork, leaded windows, high chimneys, and a thatched roof. The proprietor, alerted to their predicament, sent servants out to meet them and usher Her Grace straight up to her apartment.

"I suggest you both jump into a hot bath, to prevent taking a chill," Macheath said, after escorting them to their rooms.

"I find a tot of brandy helps," Her Grace replied, lifting a questioning eyebrow to see if this illegal beverage was available.

Macheath nodded. "Rooney keeps a bottle on hand — for medicinal purposes. Wine or tea for you, Miss Harkness?"

On an impulse, she said, "Brandy for me as well, Captain."

She hardly knew what made her say it. She disliked brandy. It was the way Macheath was taking over. The sensible thing would be to continue the few miles to Chertsey. Their hostess would understand their disarray when she heard their tale. Really the duchess was behaving very oddly.

Macheath gave a start at Marianne's answer. "Are you sure?" he asked.

"Quite sure, thank you."

"From the quantity of tea you badgered Ned for, I took you for a tea drinker," he said, examining her with suspicious interest.

"I was hoping to relieve Ned of his pistol," she replied.

"Ho, she is a regular tea granny," the duchess said. "However, after such an ordeal as you have put us through this day, a glass of well-watered brandy will do her the world of good."

"I'll have your drinks sent up," Macheath said before exiting.

When the door shut behind him, Marianne sighed. She knew her duty was to help the duchess with her bath before taking care of herself. So she was pleasantly surprised when a few moments later two maid-servants accompanied the men carrying the water abovestairs.

"The captain says we're to help you with your bath, ladies."

"That was well done," the duchess said. "Now you won't have to wait until I am finished to have yours, Marianne. I suggest you get out of that damp gown at once. You look for the world like a drowned cat. And so do I, I daresay."

"I don't need any help," Marianne said. She was accustomed to taking care of herself and knew she would be uncomfortable with someone helping her undress.

The duchess, who always relished having as many people at her beck and call as possible, at once took charge of both maids.

Marianne was still in the bath when her trunk arrived. She had begun by washing the mud from her hair. Next she washed her body and luxuriated awhile in the warm, relaxing tub, grateful to have a quiet moment to herself. Fully bathed, she wrapped herself in a soft bath sheet and opened the trunk. One of the maids came to take her soiled clothes belowstairs for cleaning. She toweled her hair as dry as she could.

Because her traveling suit was a shambles, she wore her second best gown, a sarcenet of Wedgwood blue that matched her eyes, with a white lace fichu at the throat. The silk stockings, a rare treat purchased especially for the wedding, felt luxurious as she slid them on. The blue kid slippers went with both this gown and her wedding outfit. When she was dressed, she arranged her hair at the toilet table. After its washing, it glinted coppery in the candlelight. The dampness turned it to a mass of curly tendrils that billowed like a cloud around her face. Her eyes glowed with excitement. She was "in looks," as her mistress would say.

As she ran the comb through her curls, she wondered if Macheath would be dining with them. Nothing seemed impossible on this bizarre day. What was he up to? He must know the duchess could and would report him as soon as she was up and about. Why did he not run while he had the chance? Perhaps he had already left. If so, it was gentlemanly of him to have helped them before leaving, but she regretted that he couldn't see her now. The last time he had seen her she looked like a drowned cat.

When she went through the adjoining door to the duchess's room she saw Her Grace lying in bed, dressed in her nightgown. She looked every one of her eighty-two years. Her pale face was lined and drawn; her eyes were hagged. Marianne knew then that they would be dining right here. The duchess would take a tray on her lap in bed, and Marianne would sit at the little desk by the window. Macheath would not see her looking pretty.

The brandy arrived at the door, a bottle with just one glass. A teapot and one cup were on the tray as well.

"The captain said you would prefer tea, ma'am," the servant said to Marianne.

Anger warred with pleasure, for while she much preferred tea, she resented that the captain had taken this last chance to show his power over her.

"Quite right. You are too young for brandy," the duchess said, apparently forgetting that she had approved it. She took a sip of her brandy neat and smacked her lips in approval. "I shall have a piece of chicken and some bread in my room in an hour," she said to the servant. "That is all I want tonight. These weary bones need rest."

"The same for me," Marianne said, fighting down her disappointment.

During the intervening hour, Marianne wrote a note to the countess who was to have been their hostess at Chertsey, saying they would not be stopping after all and apologizing for the inconvenience.

"No need to give a reason," the duchess said.

Marianne sat with her mistress, listening to a deal of complaining and nonsense. As the brandy in the bottle lowered, the old lady became more rambling and voluble. Macheath was a villain one moment and a hero the next. The duchess could think of nothing but him. It was much the way Marianne felt herself.

"You know what he is about, of course," the duchess said. "He thinks to humor me by these attentions so that I shan't report him. A free room and a glass of brandy will not pay for my diamonds, however. I shall speak to the constable first thing in the morning."

"Why not send for him tonight?"

"I am giving Macheath a chance to repent and do the right thing, Marianne. I am not one to hold a grudge. If he returns the necklace, I shan't report him. I think it is what he has in mind. I have brought him to see the error of his ways. Why else did he keep harping on it earlier? You recall his warning of highwaymen. It is obviously preying on his mind. There is some good in the lad yet. A pity such a handsome young whelp has gone to the bad. How easily he bore me over the water in his strong arms. If only he were not a thief — and if I were fifty years younger." She sighed and took another sip of the strong brandy. "Good stuff. It is not diluted with caramel water as I get in Bath."

The dinner tray arrived and Marianne settled in for exactly the sort of evening she would have at home, except that here she sat at the desk instead of the duchess's table. The duchess gobbled down her meal in a minute. When it was gone, she said, "Now for a little reading."

It was Marianne's cue to pick up the current journal and read to her. The duchess's eyes were not strong enough for reading by candlelight.

"Bother, we don't have a journal. Nip downstairs and get one, Marianne. They will have some at the clerk's desk. And inquire how my carriage and team are coming along, while you are there."

Marianne welcomed the chance to get out of the room. She saw the other guests just going down to dinner, ladies and gentlemen dressed in their evening finery. The low-cut gowns looked immodest to Marianne. The gentlemen's shirt collars were too high, their jackets nipped in too sharply at the waists. But Bath was a city of elderly folks. This must be the fashion in London. Macheath did not wear such exaggerated jackets, though. She did not see Macheath. She got the journal and asked the clerk if he would send to the stable to see how the duchess's rig and team were progressing.

The companion of a duchess was treated with respect. The George and Dragon did not get many noble customers.

"Have a seat while you are waiting, ma'am," he said, indicating a row of aging upholstered chairs by the wall.

She sat down and entertained herself by watching the guests come and go. It was strange they were all couples, mostly youngish. There were no older pairs, no families with children, no old bachelors or spinsters. Perhaps there was some sort of party going on. She was still there five minutes later when the front door opened and Macheath stepped in.

He was dressed for evening in a bronze velvet jacket with a tumble of lace at the cuffs and looked not only handsome but distinguished beside the other guests. A certain air of dignity, of what she could only call breeding, hung about him. It was there not only in his toilette but in his walk, which was self-confident without being a swagger. In the folds of his cravat a yellow stone, topaz or yellow diamond, twinkled. A long greatcoat the color of sand, cut in the new Spanish style called a Wellington mantle after the hero of the Peninsular War, lay open. Another change of clothes confirmed that he lived nearby. When he saw her, Macheath stopped and stared, then rushed forward.

"Miss Harkness! What are you doing down here alone? I hope nothing is wrong."

"No indeed, Captain. I came to pick up a journal to read to the duchess. I am just waiting for word on how the carriage and team are doing."

"You shouldn't be alone in a place like this."

"But it is a perfectly respectable inn — is it not?"

"It is not exactly the Clarendon," he said, mentioning one of the finer London hotels. "I shall stay with you until the clerk returns. I daresay the duchess is eager to be on her way, eh?"

"She is. I would have thought you would be gone long since yourself, Captain. This cannot be a healthy place for you."

"I came to have a word with Her Grace before leaving. Has she reported me to the constable yet?" He didn't sound frightened, only curious.

"She plans to do it first thing in the morning, before we leave."

"Why did she wait?"

"I believe she wanted to speak to you before doing it."

"I'll have a word with her now — as soon as the clerk returns."

The clerk returned shortly to report that the carriage was not damaged and the horse's leg had been poulticed. Beeton felt that it could continue on its way tomorrow, if he went at a slow pace.

"Shall we go upstairs now?" Macheath said and took Marianne's arm to accompany her across the lobby.

A few heads turned to watch the young couple. For the thirty seconds it took to traverse the lobby, Marianne felt like one of the fortunate ladies she had been envying, with a handsome beau or husband on her arm.

"You didn't tell me whether you enjoyed your tea, Miss Harkness," Macheath said with a quizzing smile.

"Why did you change my order?"

"You are too young and innocent for the dissipation of brandy. That is a brew for scoundrels — and duchesses. I felt I might be the cause of it. I have enough regrets, without that," he said rather wistfully.

His tone and the way he looked at her suggested he was sorry for the trouble he had caused her. She waited a moment, but when he didn't say more, she tapped on the duchess's door and stepped in. The duchess's health had deteriorated further since Marianne had left. Her face, twisted into a grimace of pain, was a ghastly gray shade. The blankets were in a knot as she writhed on the bed.

"Oh my God! She's had an attack!"

Macheath took one searching look at her and said, "No, she's sick to her stomach."

He grabbed the tin wastebasket by the desk and rushed forward. He helped the duchess into a sitting position as she leaned over the basket and cast up her accounts. When she had emptied her stomach, she collapsed against the pillows to catch her breath.

"I have been poisoned," she said a moment later in a feeble voice. "It must have been in the brandy. You aren't feeling sick, Marianne?"

"No, I'm fine."

Macheath glanced at the nearly empty bottle. "How much did you drink?" he asked.

"Only a few sips," she lied.

"About eight ounces, to judge by the bottle. You're lucky you didn't poison yourself."

He rang for a servant and put the offending waste-basket in the hall. Marianne bathed the duchess's face and tried to make her comfortable.

"Shall I call a doctor?" she asked her mistress.

"I believe I can sleep now. There was something I wanted to say to Macheath."

"I wanted to speak to you as well, Duchess."

"Tomorrow," she said with a deep sigh. "Call on me tomorrow, Captain. I am too tired now."

"We'll leave you," he replied, and taking Marianne's elbow, he led her through the adjoining door to her room.

"Thank you again, Captain," Marianne said. "How did you know what ailed her?"

"I've seen more than a few men in the same state."

"I wonder what else you have seen," she said, gazing at him bemusedly.

His dark eyes sparkled into hers. His fingers brushed up her arm from her elbow to settle on her shoulder with an engrossing intimacy. "Many sights of wonder

— but I never before saw a girl like you, Marianne," he said softly. Then he closed the door, and she was alone with him.

CHAPTER
NINE

Marianne felt a wild fluttering in her breast. She told herself it was fear, perfectly natural fear at being alone with a criminal, but she didn't fool herself. Those eyes glowing softly into hers held a different sort of danger.

She schooled her voice to calmness and said, "It would be best to leave the door open in case Her Grace wants me," and opened the door.

She peeked across to the duchess's canopied bed and saw by the flickering light of the lamp that her eyes were closed. The stertorous snorts were already beginning, indicating a peaceful sleep. It would be the effect of the brandy.

"There goes that excuse," Macheath said with a devilish grin.

"I shall get the journal. I might as well read it until bedtime." She took a step forward. Macheath put his hand on her arm to detain her. His fingers felt like a branding iron.

"I have a different idea," he suggested. "It is not yet nine o'clock. Let us go below and have dinner."

"I have already had dinner, Captain," she replied in a prim voice that tried to conceal her interest. But the flush on her cheeks and the gleam in her eyes betrayed it. The fingers on her arm loosened and she drew her arm away.

"You call a chicken leg and a crust of bread dinner, after your strenuous day? I saw your tray in the other room."

"You don't miss much!"

"I missed my dinner. I had planned to invite you and the duchess to join me in my parlor, but by the time I arrived, the duchess was already in bed. You could keep me company, have a glass of wine while I eat. Come now, you are all dressed up. Confess you would like to go downstairs and show off that charming gown." He spoke of the gown, but it was her face, with its halo of shining curls, that he gazed at — with a long, lingering perusal of her eyes and lips — until she felt warm and unaccountably nervous.

"I shouldn't leave Her Grace."

"She's sound asleep!"

"She might awaken."

"Not for several hours yet. There's a bell cord by her bed. She has only to give it a pull and a servant will come running."

Marianne wavered under the force of temptation. Familiar with her Bible, she knew how Eve must have felt in the Garden of Eden. The duchess would sleep until morning. It was not quite nine o'clock. She did not usually retire before eleven. She could sit alone, reading the journal and listening to the duchess snore, or she could go below and spend an hour with an extremely handsome, dashing highwayman who made her feel beautiful and desirable for the first time in her life. She would not dare to do such a thing in Bath, where all the old cats knew her and would gossip, but no one knew her here. Being on holiday seemed to relax the rules of acceptable behavior.

He saw she was wavering, and to convince her he said, "I have something I would like to discuss with you, Marianne. Something important."

The "Marianne" seemed to lend a new familiarity, almost an intimacy, to their acquaintance. She remembered the duchess's words, that Macheath might want to return the diamonds. "Something important" sounded as if she could be right. If this was the case, Marianne had something important she wished to say to him as well. She might be able to talk him out of this sinful life he led. It seemed wrong to refuse such a possibility of reforming a criminal.

"Very well," she said, "but I should leave Her Grace a note, in case she awakens and I am not here. She will be worried, you know."

"By all means, leave her a note." He reached in his pocket and handed her a pencil, drew out a note-book, and tore off a sheet.

Marianne wrote in perfect copperplate, "Your Grace: I have gone downstairs to have a word with Captain Macheath. I shan't be long. Marianne." She tiptoed into the next room and put the note on the bedside table under the lamp, turned the wick down low, and tiptoed back to her room.

"Aren't you going to lock your door?" he asked as they left.

"Oh, should I? I don't have anything worth stealing. I never stayed at an inn before. Since I've been grown-up, I mean."

"There are people who would steal the buttons off your nightgown."

She gave him a pert grin. "True, but as you will be with me, where is the danger?"

He clamped his hand to his heart and cried, "Touched to the quick!" in melodramatic accents. "Still, best to be sure. I am not the only highwayman on the prowl. We'll lock the duchess's room as well."

She returned and got the keys from the duchess's toilet table. Macheath locked both doors and they went downstairs. He led her through the lobby to a snug little private parlor with a cozy fire blazing in the grate and a table laid for three. This reassured her that he had intended to include the duchess in the invitation, and made her more comfortable. The lamps were turned down low. She glanced around at the hunting prints on the wall, the indifferent carpet on the floor, and the miniature sideboard holding pewter plates and some dishes.

A bottle of red wine was open on the table. Macheath showed her to a seat and poured two glasses. A waiter came to the parlor to take their orders.

"They do an excellent beefsteak here," he tempted. "Why don't you try a little?"

"I'll have dessert with you later," she said.

"A sweet tooth, eh? I suspected as much. My sister is the same."

"You have a sister!" she exclaimed.

"Two, along with a mama and, once upon a time, a papa, though I don't remember him well. Did you think I was hatched from an egg in a cuckoo's nest?"

Macheath's having sisters seemed to normalize him in some manner Marianne couldn't quite comprehend. "I'm an only child," she said vaguely.

As soon as the servant left, she said, "What are your sisters like, Captain?"

"The younger, Meggie, is rather like you. The older, Eleanor, is more like me. The black ewe of the family," he added. "As both are still in the schoolroom, however, there may be time to reform Eleanor yet."

The word "reform" reminded Marianne of why she was here. "You said you wanted to discuss something important, Captain."

"I did. I do, but let us enjoy dinner first, become a little acquainted. All I know about you is that you are an orphan and act as the duchess's companion and dogsbody. It cannot be a pleasant life for such a young lady."

"Young! Why thank you, sir. I am one-and-twenty."

"That old?" he said, chewing back a smile. "I would not have taken you for a day over eighteen."

"Well, thank you. As to your comment, my life is not precisely pleasant, but it is not unpleasant, either. It could be worse. I used to live with my parents in Somerset. Papa raised cattle. Mama died when I was sixteen. My father took to drink and gambling. When he drank himself to death a year later, there was no money. The estate, heavily mortgaged, was sold to pay his debts. The duchess is not actually kin, just a connection by marriage. She offered me the position I now hold. I feel fortunate to have it. I believe you have a more exciting story, Captain?"

"As my pockets were to let, I decided to make my career in the army. My uncle bought me a cornet, and I went to Spain to fight with Wellington."

"Was it Spanish you and your servant were speaking the night you held us up? I know it was not French."

"Yes, it allows us to talk in front of our victims without being understood."

"Surely Miguel is not Spanish, though? He has a hint of brogue in his speech."

"There was a woman in Spain who used to call him that. The other soldiers took up the name in fun, and it has stuck. He was my batman and is now my factotum — and friend."

"That scar on his cheek —"

"*Badajos*," he said briefly. "Unlike many of my men, Miguel and I escaped with not only our lives but with all our limbs."

The servant returned with dinner. While he arranged it, Macheath said a few words to him. When they were alone again, Marianne frowned and said, "I daresay shooting and killing begin to seem natural after a few years in the army."

"It is kind of you to look for an excuse for me, but the shooting and killing never seemed natural or normal or anything but barbaric to me. Even in my work now, I only shoot above the head to frighten people, unless they shoot first, as Beeton did. Miguel is an excellent shot. He could have killed or maimed Tom.

He only winged his arm, to stop him from shooting at us. There was not that much shooting in the Peninsula, actually. For weeks on end we would march through the dust or sit waiting in the broiling sun, then a few hours or days of killing and burying the dead, and it would be another long wait. To pass the time, we had the pleasure of writing to wives and mothers and fathers to tell them their loved ones were dead. I was a foolish, romantic boy when I joined up. I didn't see beyond the scarlet regimentals and travel to an exotic land to stop Boney from taking over the world."

"I see why you did not wish to discuss this during dinner," she said, and immediately changed the subject. "Before you joined the army, where did you live?"

"In Kent."

While he ate, he spoke a little of his youth there, urged on by leading questions. It sounded a happy, carefree sort of life. Riding, hunting, shooting, fishing, lessons of course, and as he grew older dancing and social visits were added to his entertainments. An occasional detail suggested to Marianne that he came from a wealthier background than she did. He mentioned a horse his uncle was training for Ascot. Another time, he spoke of a ball his mama held for one hundred and fifty guests, half of them staying overnight. It would take a large house and a great number of servants to manage such a crowd.

His table manners were good. His speech, too, was that of a well-born, well-educated gentleman. What could account for his descent into the criminal class?

When he had finished his beefsteak, the servant returned and they ordered dessert. Apple tart and cheese for Macheath, a cream bun for Marianne.

Over coffee, she tried to revert to his experiences in the war, but Macheath had no more to say on the subject.

"It is best forgotten," he said, "I am home, alive, in one piece, unlike many friends."

"Very well, then let us proceed to the really interesting part. Why did you turn highwayman? What you have told me suggests your family is not without means and influence. Could they not have found you a suitable position?"

"I have an inheritance," he said. "I don't take the money for myself, Marianne. I mentioned being more fortunate than many of my fellow soldiers. They have come home crippled, maimed, unable to earn a living for themselves and their families." As he spoke, an angry bitterness crept into his tone. "They should be heroes, but they receive only a miserable pittance of a pension. When they are unable to work their tenant farms, they are turned off to starve. When you get to London, you will see them on crutches, begging on street corners — men who risked their lives for England. And the chosen few who stayed home, getting fat on the war, begrudge them their pension. I am very choosy as to whom I rob. I take only from those who can well afford it, preferably those who profited from the war."

"And do you give the money to these unfortunate veterans?"

"Of course!" he said, offended that she should ask. "That is the whole point of it."

"But the duchess was not one of those profiteers who made money from the war."

"The duchess was a mistake. I was waiting for the Duke of Ancaster. I had word he would be passing that way. He made thousands manufacturing arms for the war. A tithe of it should go back to those who need a crust of bread more than he needs another horse or carriage or mistress. When I saw the strawberry leaves on the duchess's coach, I thought she was Ancaster and attacked. Then Tom shot at us, and Miguel returned fire. I lost my temper and decided the duchess should contribute to my cause. She can well afford it."

"That first night, the night you robbed the duchess, you went out again after Ancaster?"

"Yes."

"And you got him?"

"I did."

"Good!" When she realized what she had said, she gave a gasp of dismay. "Not that two wrongs make a right! And it is very dangerous, Captain."

"I have friends who help me, hide me if I am chased, or would give me an alibi if required. Ned is one of them. He lost a son in Spain. There are others."

"You have risked your life once — in the Peninsula, I mean. Now it is someone else's turn."

"The devil of it is, no one seems eager to take his turn."

"Could something not be done in Parliament? With your connections, you could be a member of Parliament yourself and lead a crusade."

"It is something to think about. I was so furious when I first returned to England and saw how the men were treated that I wanted to take direct action. It is true, one man can't do it all."

"Was there anything else you wished to speak about?"

"Many things, Marianne," he said, reaching across the table and squeezing her fingers. "But you are referring to business. I hoped to strike a bargain with the duchess regarding her necklace. I shouldn't have taken it. I shall have a word with her tomorrow morning." He looked a question at her.

Marianne smiled softly. "I think you will find her reasonable."

"I shall expect you to put in a good word for me."

"You may be sure I will. And now I really must get back to her. But I am glad I came."

"I am flattered that you prefer my conversation to her snoring. I hope you have some cotton to stuff in your ears."

They rose and reluctantly left the cozy parlor.

CHAPTER
TEN

They went back upstairs. The captain unlocked Marianne's door and handed her the keys.

Before going in, she said, "Are you a captain? A real captain, I mean?"

"Why no, ma'am. I am a colonel."

"Oh, you are joking, Macheath. I know that's not your real name." She looked a question at him. He just shook his head, unwilling to tell her who he was.

"Shall we just have a look at Her Grace before I leave?" he suggested.

"Yes, that's a good idea." She listened a moment. "I don't hear any snoring. Oh dear, I hope she is all right."

She hastened through the adjoining door to see the duchess lying at her ease. Her breathing was normal. She had turned on her side, which might account for the interruption of snoring. Marianne retrieved her note and put it in her pocket. She saw no reason to tell the duchess of her outing.

"She's fine," she said when she rejoined the captain. "It has been an enjoyable evening, Captain." Wishing to establish something like friendship, she offered him her hand.

He took it and drew her closer to him. His hands were on her shoulders. She felt she should draw away but was mesmerized by those dark eyes glittering into hers, drawing closer, closer, until they were a shimmering blur, and his lips brushed hers, soft as the flutter of a moth's wing. They grazed across her cheek to her ear.

"So sweet," he murmured, and kissed her ear, while Marianne stood, not breathing, until her lungs felt they would burst.

She didn't make a move to stop him or encourage him. It seemed something outside of her control. When she didn't withdraw, the captain lifted his head and gazed at her a moment with a deep, penetrating look, and she stared back, unblinking, waiting. His arms went around her, his head lowered to hers. And from the next room came an angry shout from the duchess.

"Well, that is certainly a help," the captain snorted. Then he laughed. "So much for romance."

"I had best see what she wants."

"I'll go with you and speak to her now."

"And let her know you were in my room? Wait a moment, then go outside and tap on her door from the hallway."

His eyebrows lifted in surprise. "You're well organized. Have you done this before?"

Marianne was already on her way to the adjoining door. She just looked her objection to this risqué suggestion over her shoulder. She found the duchess sitting up in bed, yanking at the coverlet and scowling.

"What kept you? There is someone knocking on my door. See who it is. The knocking woke me up."

Marianne hastened to the door, preparing a surprised expression to greet Macheath. A short man with a pale, narrow face and dark, deep-set eyes stepped in. He was wearing a dun-colored redingote that brushed his ankles and carrying a curled beaver.

"Officer Bruce, of Bow Street, madam," he said. "I am here on behalf of the Duke of Ancaster. I would like to have a word with Her Grace."

Bow Street! Marianne looked around the hall but saw no sign of Macheath.

"Ancaster?" the duchess called from her bed. "What does he want with me?"

Officer Bruce strode to her bedside. "We want your assistance, madam. He was robbed not far from here last night by a highwayman. We believe it is the royal scamp known as Captain Jack. My investigations have led me to this inn. I have heard belowstairs that you, too, were robbed. Of a diamond necklace is my information. Am I right or am I right?"

"Quite right," she said. "I mentioned it to the gels who helped me when I arrived. I planned to report it to the constable tomorrow. As you can see, the shock has driven me to my bed. What did the scoundrel take from Ancaster?"

"Three thousand pounds in cash. Rent monies that he was taking to London to pay his bills."

"The man is a fool, traveling with such a sum."

"That's as may be, Your Grace. Some would say 'tis foolish to travel with diamonds. What can you tell me of this Captain Jack?"

"He robbed me of a diamond necklace worth five thousand pounds."

"Can you describe the man?"

"He wore a mask. He was a big man."

Marianne stood with her heart in her mouth. She wished she could indicate to the duchess that Macheath intended to return the diamonds. As this was impossible, she hoped that Macheath was listening at the door and would have the sense to get on Juno and ride as fast and as far as he could.

As she stood, sweating at every pore, another knock sounded at the door. She went to answer it and saw Macheath standing in the doorway. Officer Bruce saw him, too. She wanted to warn him away, but before she could do it, he spoke.

"Is Her Grace awake?" he asked. "Ah, I see she is, and entertaining company," he said in a drawling voice unlike his own. He walked into the room and directed a long stare at the duchess.

"So, it is you," she said in a gloating voice.

"As you see. I have come to pay my respects, and see if there is anything I can do for you before I go out for the evening, ma'am."

"This is Officer Bruce, from Bow Street," she said with a wicked smile. "He is looking for the thief who stole my diamonds. He wants a description of the fellow."

"A young man, I believe you said?" Macheath drawled, and brushed an invisible speck of lint from his jacket. "Tall, well built."

Her smile stretched to a triumphant grin. "I would not say well built. About your own size. An awkward, ungainly fellow," she said spitefully.

"Just so."

"And who would this gentleman be?" Bruce inquired, examining Macheath with sharp interest.

"Oh, you have not met," the duchess said, staring at Macheath like a cat playing with a mouse. "Remiss of me."

Marianne stood in an agony of suspense. Her mistress was enjoying this little charade. Marianne looked at Macheath and saw the tension in his smile. His hands, which he now held behind his back, had white knuckles.

"This is my nephew Ronald Fitz-Matthew. He is accompanying me to London," the duchess announced.

Marianne felt the tension melt out of her joints as she exhaled softly.

Officer Bruce turned to Macheath. "Were you with Her Grace when she was robbed, sir?"

"Alas, no, or I would have put a bullet through the bounder. I had arranged to meet my aunt here this afternoon."

"Pity. Can you tell me, Your Grace, what sort of nag was he riding?"

"An Arabian stallion, a fine mount."

"That's odd, then. Ancaster said it was a bay mare."

"It was dark. Perhaps Ancaster was mistaken," she said.

"I shouldn't think so. The duke knows horseflesh."

"Are you suggesting I don't?" the duchess snapped.

"Nay now, milady. No need to get yourself riled up. No doubt it was a different lad that got hold of you. This area close to London has two dozen scamps on the prowl. Another time, you want to travel in a caravan of three or more rigs, with plenty of mounted guards. They think twice before attacking a caravan. Captain Jack don't usually prey on ladies. He has a preference for well-inlaid gents. I'll take a description of your sparklers to circulate about London. If they show up, we'll return them to you."

She gave a detailed description of the necklace and gave the address in London where she could be reached: Grosvenor Square, the residence of the Dowager Countess of Thornleigh.

"It is a shame and a disgrace that Bow Street cannot protect honest citizens," she continued. "Why are you wasting your time here harassing old ladies? Get out and find my diamonds. Now leave me. I am tired."

"Thank you for your help, madam. Perhaps you'd join me for a drink downstairs, Mr Fitz-Matthew? I'd like a word with you as well."

"That is *Sir* Ronald Fitz-Matthew," Macheath replied in that languid, drawling voice. "I would be happy to assist you in any way I can. Shocking the way these scamps rule the roads. It is interesting you mentioned a bay mare. I saw a sly-looking rogue riding such a mount this very night. He was dressed all in black, wearing a strange sort of slouch hat."

"That sounds like Captain Jack! How long ago? Which way was he going?"

Macheath opened the door and ushered Officer Bruce out. At the door he turned and blew a kiss to the duchess. "I shall see you tomorrow morning, Aunt. Sleep tight."

After he had left, the duchess uttered a harsh laugh. "There is a brass box for you!"

"Why did you do it?" Marianne asked.

The duchess bridled up. "Since when do I have to explain myself to you, miss?" She sniffed and grappled with her shawl for a moment, then said, "Since you ask, Macheath has had ample time to get rid of the necklace. Bow Street will never find it, but Macheath is now indebted to me. Naturally he will return the necklace to repay me for protecting him."

Marianne studied the raddled old face, which was showing signs of embarrassment. She sensed it was not only the duchess's hope of getting her diamonds back that had caused her to protect Macheath. She liked him. She was going to make Macheath her new pet. Marianne could almost feel sorry for him.

"I see," she said. "Is there anything I can do for you before I retire?"

"Pour me a glass of wine. And put a sign on my door that I do not wish to be disturbed again. Now off with you. Best have a glass of wine yourself as well. It will help you sleep."

Marianne did as requested, then went back to her own room, where she sat, recovering from the strain of the Bow Street officer's visit. What an exciting, dangerous life Macheath led. But sooner or later, he would be caught. Not all his victims would be so obliging as the duchess.

She was too upset to go to bed immediately. She settled in by the grate to drink her wine. She was just about to undress for bed when a light scratching came at the door. Not a knock, just a scratching sound. She knew it was Macheath even before she asked.

"It's me. Can I see you for a moment?"

She opened the door and he stepped just inside it. "What possessed her to do it?" he asked.

"She says you'll have to give her back her diamonds now. You are in her debt."

"I wish I had done it before Bow Street got here. I came back to thank her, but I see she is sporting her oak."

"Yes, she's sleeping. What did you say to Officer Bruce?"

"I believe I convinced him Captain Jack is busy elsewhere this evening. I have volunteered to ride out with him and lend a hand in any arrest that might occur. I told him I wanted to pick up my pistol before leaving."

"You are shameless, Captain."

"You can call me Sir Ronald."

"You will have to pay more than the diamonds for this favor, you know."

"What an intriguing threat. Surely the old girl isn't on the lookout for a husband? A bit long in the tooth for my taste."

"Not quite that bad, but don't be surprised if she takes to flirting with you."

"Hussy," he said, grinning. "Now if it were her companion I was required to court, that would be more agreeable. *En effet*, a distinct pleasure, madam."

He lifted her fingers to his lips and was gone. Marianne paused a moment, staring at the spot where he had stood. Then she slowly locked the door, not thinking, but feeling the tingle of blood through her veins as she considered this flirtatious speech.

CHAPTER
ELEVEN

It was late in the night when Marianne awoke in the unfamiliar room, wondering at that first blink where she was. As the recent past came back to her, she listened for the duchess's snoring. All was silent in the next room. She was already out of bed and on her way to the door when she heard the faint voice calling, "Marianne. Are you there?"

"What is it, Your Grace?" she asked. The lamp was burning low, showing her the duchess's raddled face.

"I am famished," the duchess said in a querulous voice.

"The kitchen will be closed by now. It's not long until morning."

"I know, I know, but I cannot sleep a wink for the hunger pangs. I lost my dinner, you recall. I have been ringing the bell this past half hour trying to rouse someone belowstairs. There is no answer."

"What do you want me to do?" Marianne asked, though she already knew the answer.

"Would you mind running below and asking the fellow on the desk to heat me a glass of milk?" It was not really a question, it was a polite command. "I shall make do with that until morning. There is bound to be someone at the desk, if not in the kitchen."

"Very well," Marianne said.

Her watch showed her it was three-thirty. She could not go belowstairs in her nightgown. To avoid getting dressed, she put on her mantle and fastened it around her shoulders. Lamps burned low at either end of the hallway. She chased her shadow along to the staircase and hastened down. There was a man at the desk, snoozing with his hand in his chin. She gave the bell a light ring to rouse him.

He shook his head. "Ah, miss — er — the duchess's companion, is it not?"

"Miss Harkness, yes. Her Grace has not been well. She is having trouble sleeping. Could you have someone heat her up a glass of milk?"

"The kitchen help are all in bed, Miss Harkness. We're only a small establishment. We can't keep the kitchen open twenty-four hours a day. Cook will be back on duty in a couple of hours. I am not allowed to leave my post or I'd do it myself. There is money here, you know, that someone might walk off with." He glanced behind him to a strongbox on a shelf.

"Oh." She looked at him helplessly. "Her Grace is really very hungry."

"You are perfectly welcome to heat the milk up yourself, if you like. The cook leaves the fire banked. There is milk aplenty in the larder. The kitchen is just at the foot of the staircase, there at the end of the passage." He pointed across the empty lobby to an archway and a corridor beyond.

Marianne hesitated only a moment. Neither she nor the duchess would get any further rest unless she had her milk. "Thank you," she said and ran across the lobby, down a pair of dark stairs to the kitchen.

It was much larger than she was accustomed to, with three stoves standing side by side. Everything was neat and tidy, with the fires banked as the clerk had said. There was a large, uncurtained window looking out on the back. She felt exposed, but it was not likely that anyone would be there at this hour of the morning. She forgot about it as she hurriedly gathered up a small pan and arranged it on the stove. That door there on the left must be the larder. She had no trouble finding what she needed. She decided to heat a glass of milk for herself while she was at it. She watched as the milk began to simmer. She was just about to fetch two glasses from the rack above the sink when the back door flew open.

There had been no warning. No sound of approaching footsteps, no shadow at the window, no rattle of the doorknob. One moment she was alone, and the next moment a stocky, rough, unkempt-looking man in a black jacket was in the room, staring at her from a pair of sharp black eyes. Wisps of black hair stuck out from under a misshapen black hat.

"A new cook, then?" he said, swaggering forward with his shoulders back. "I haven't seen you before, have I, my darling?"

She sensed his intention even before he touched her. It was there, in his bold, darting eyes, his loose grin, and his swaggering gait. "Give me a kiss, love," he said, sliding his arm around her waist. At close range, she could smell the stench of the stables from him.

"Let go of me," she said, trying to pull away. "I am not the cook."

"Serving wench, then. Stealing Cook's milk. She'll give you what for."

Marianne was frightened but not yet terrified. In the past, she had found the duchess's name a sovereign shield against unwanted familiarity. "I am a guest here, sir. I am traveling with the Duchess of Bixley."

A throaty chuckle was his reaction to that. "Ye must take me for a Johnny Raw. A duchess at this place. Aye, you're a duchess's lady-in-waiting, and I'm the Archbishop of Canterbury."

On this disbelieving jeer he put both arms around her and tried to kiss her. She pushed him away as best she could, but he had the strength of a tiger and the tenacity of a bulldog. His rough hands pulled her mantle aside, revealing what was obviously a nightgown. When he saw this, a lecherous smile split his face.

"I'll have you right here on the floor, my pretty."

Marianne's heart began banging against her ribs. Her breaths were coming in short pants. As she looked wildly around her for a weapon, she espied the milk on the stove, just about to bubble over. She reached for it and dashed it in his face. Most of it landed on his hat, but some got in his eyes. He let out a yelp and brushed the boiling milk from his face. While he was distracted, she turned to run. The man got hold of the end of her mantle and pulled her back. She stumbled and fell

100

against the edge of the table. He reached out, wearing an ugly leer, pulled her mantle until it came loose, and threw it on the floor.

"Ye'll pay for that, minx!" he said in a fierce, growling tone.

Marianne looked wildly around for a poker or a knife, or some weapon more deadly than the small, empty milk pan she still held in her hand. It didn't occur to her to scream. She was too frightened. She did hear the welcome rushing down the stairs of a man's feet, however, and gasped in relief. It would be the clerk, risking his money box a moment to see if she had found what she required. Her assailant didn't loosen his hold, but he looked alert at the sound of the intruder.

When he saw who it was, his eyes widened. "Macheath!" he cried.

Marianne looked and saw the captain, whom she scarcely recognized. He was wearing his black mask and hat and the black jacket he had been wearing the night he robbed the duchess. A pistol in his right hand was aimed at her assailant. She saw his finger twitch with the instinct to fire it.

"Don't!" she cried. "Don't kill him, Captain."

Macheath's eyes never left the assailant. He walked forward, raised his other hand and with its outer edge slashed the man on the side of his neck. The man fell in a heap at his feet. Marianne dropped the pan, which rattled on the brick floor. Macheath put his pistol in the waist of his trousers, delved into the man's pockets, and withdrew a jingling bag of coins, which he transferred to his own pocket. Then he picked the man up by the scruff of the neck, heaved him out the back door, and locked it, before turning back to Marianne.

"What the devil are you doing here?" he demanded.

"The duchess wanted some milk," she said, and burst into tears. She was not prone to tears, but in the aftermath of her frightening experience, she couldn't seem to control them. Her shoulders shook with the deep, wrenching sobs.

Macheath saw her mantle cast aside on the floor, saw the spilled milk, and had a good idea what had happened. He hardly knew whether he was angrier with Dirty Dick McGinty, the duchess, himself, or Marianne. No, not with Marianne. She looked twelve years old in her long flannelette nightgown, with her hair hanging about her face as she tried to hiccup the tears away.

He picked up the mantle and put it around her shoulders, then folded her in his arms to soothe her hysteria. He felt her body trembling and held her closer, till his body heat began to ease her shivering. As his fingers moved gently through the silken tousle of her curls, he felt a fierce well of protectiveness rise within him. It was outrageous that this vulnerable girl was sent down here alone in the middle of the night, with the likes of Dirty Dick on the prowl.

"It's all right. It's all right, my dear," he said, gently stroking her shoulders.

"He was going to —"

"I know. I know, Marianne. It's over now. You shouldn't have been here alone. Did he hurt you?"

102

She lifted her head and gazed at him through tear-dimmed eyes. "You came just in time, Captain." Macheath's heart swelled at the look on her face, which was close to adoration, and shrank again as the look dwindled to a frown. "I wish you would take that mask off," she said. He drew it down. "How did you come — why are you here? Have you been out robbing coaches again?"

"No, I have been with Officer Bruce, looking for myself in all the wrong places. I left him at another inn, where I heard a rumor McGinty was encroaching on my territory. I decided to teach him a lesson. I knew he would come here."

She drew back and gazed up at him. "Why? Why would he come here?"

"It is that sort of place."

"A highwaymen's den?" she asked in disbelief. "But I saw many fine ladies."

"You saw highwaymen's doxies, dressed up in stolen finery."

"Why did you bring us to a place like this?"

Macheath was annoyed at the change in mood from adoring girl to scolding lady. "You seem to forget — you and the duchess were soaking wet, your carriage was mired in mud, and darkness was coming on. I hadn't much choice."

"You might have warned us at least!"

"How was I to know you'd be roaming about alone in the middle of the night in your nightdress."

"It's a nightgown," she said, and with an air of dignity, she pulled her mantle tightly about her. Then she ruined the effect by wiping at her tears with the back of her hand.

Macheath didn't want to argue. He wanted to see again that softly adoring look he had glimpsed a moment ago. He wanted to kiss those rosebud lips, to feel again her soft femininity trembling in his arms. He handed her his handkerchief and she dried her eyes.

"Come, I'll take you upstairs," he said, reaching for her hand. She looked at the handkerchief and put it in her pocket.

They took a step toward the staircase, then Marianne stopped. "The milk," she said. "I came down for milk. I'd best take it up or she'll be awake all night."

Macheath was glad for the excuse to be alone with her. He watched as she moved gracefully about the kitchen, finding another pan, filling it with milk, taking glasses from the shelf.

"None for me?" he asked when she placed two cups on the tray.

She tilted her head and gave him a wry smile as she added a third glass. "I didn't take you for a milk drinker. Brandy or Blue Ruin seem more like it."

"I also enjoy the simple things of life, Marianne."

"What are you going to do with McGinty?"

"Do you want me to darken his daylights, put a bullet through him? I would be happy to oblige."

"Is that the simple sort of thing you enjoy? Shooting people? I meant about the money he stole."

"Finders, keepers."

"I don't believe that refers to money found in other people's pockets, Captain."

"Depends on how it got there."

"Did you assume that whoever you robbed tonight before you came here had also stolen the money in his pockets?"

"I haven't — met any carriages this evening."

"Then why are you dressed like that? You were wearing your mask."

He gave a quizzing grin. "Masquerade party?"

"Since McGinty recognized you, what was the point of wearing it? You —" She was going to say he had promised to quit, but he hadn't actually said anything of the sort. She poured the milk. "I wish you wouldn't, Captain," she said in a small, sad voice. "You'll end up with a bullet in your heart one night."

"Would that matter to you, Marianne?"

She handed him the glass of milk. "It's always sad to see a young person die. One wonders what he might have made of his life, had he lived. You could be anything. You're smart, you're brave, strong."

He made a deprecating gesture. "Are you sure this is me you're talking about?"

"You didn't recognize the picture because I left out one feature. Stubborn."

She picked up the tray. Macheath put his glass on it and took it from her. "If you think I am going to allow you to go upstairs alone, you are very much mistaken, Miss Harkness. You attract highwaymen like honey attracts flies. And this place is full of them."

The clerk glanced at them as they passed. He didn't seem surprised that she had found an escort in the kitchen. It was that kind of place.

CHAPTER
TWELVE

"Since Her Grace is awake, I'll have a word with her now," Macheath said as they drew to a stop outside the duchess's door.

Marianne cast a questioning, hopeful look at him. His eyes met hers and held them for a long moment. The smile that spread slowly up from his lips to lighten his eyes softened her heart as no words of love could do. He looked like a young boy, eager to please his tutor. This is how Macheath must have been before war had warped his nature, giving him that hard edge that both frightened and intrigued her. Something twisted in her breast, making her feel warm and soft inside.

She didn't say anything. Words seemed inadequate, even superfluous. His eyes told her he was returning the diamonds to please her; her answering smile was all the thanks he wanted. She unlocked the door and went into the duchess's room with Macheath behind her, carrying the tray. After all her trouble, she found the duchess sound asleep.

"I'll awaken her," Marianne said.

Macheath just shook his head lightly. "Let her sleep. She needs it. All this commotion has been hard on the old girl. I'll come back in the morning. I told her I would call."

"I'll leave the milk here, in case she awakens again before morning."

She left the milk on the bedside table and they went to Marianne's room, closing the door behind them. It no longer seemed strange being alone in her room with Macheath, but it was almost painfully exciting.

He took his glass of milk and clinked it against hers. "To — us?" he suggested playfully, peering down at her to see if she objected.

"To your reformation," she parried. "Or is that hopelessly naïve of me?"

"You could reform Old Nick himself. To my reformation." They drank. "To prove it, I'll leave the diamonds with you now. You can give them to the duchess when she awakens."

"Why do you not wait and give them to her yourself?"

"I want to go home early tomorrow. I have a few things to attend to."

"Where is home?" she asked eagerly — too eagerly. It was as if a shade had been drawn over his face at hearing the question, leaving it blank.

When he spoke, even his voice was different. "Not far away, but as you are to leave tomorrow, I shall give you the necklace tonight. If I were you, I would take it and run," he said lightly.

It was a joke, of course. He just wanted to change the subject to conceal where he lived, who he was. She knew she would not learn anything he didn't want to tell her and accepted it, though she was hurt that he didn't trust her.

"Your home must be very close by, as I noticed you had changed your clothes for dinner."

"I didn't go home for that. I keep a spare set of duds in my room here. I keep a room — for emergencies. It's better you not know where I live, Marianne. You are too innocent. If Officer Bruce should decide to question you ... I am worried about you ladies having the diamonds with you in this place. I want you to take my pistol."

"I would rather not. I'd be afraid to shoot it."

"Would you not have been glad to have it tonight, when Dirty Dick was at you?"

"Perhaps. But really I would rather not. I'd probably shoot myself."

"I certainly wouldn't want that to happen. I have it! A knife! No, no. Don't look at me like that. It is not a carving knife, but a pretty little thing I picked up in Spain. Practically a fruit knife. It will fit in your reticule." He reached under his jacket, behind his back, and pulled a dainty little bone-handled knife from his waistband.

"What other lethal weapons do you carry?" she asked, taking the knife and wincing at its razor-sharp edge.

"Just a garrote and a cannon — for emergencies," he said, smiling.

She shook her head in wonder. "How on earth did I ever meet anyone like you?"

"You make me realize what a bloodthirsty monster I have become. I have been too long away from polite society."

"It's not too late to turn back, Jack."

He set his glass aside and took her hand. "That is the first time you have called me by my name. Actually, I prefer John. Jack is my nom de guerre."

"John. Yes, I prefer that, too. It's more respectable. I always think of Jack Ketch when I hear Jack."

"I have noticed your reluctance to use it. I feared it was my avocation that was keeping you at arm's length."

"It was."

His eyes brightened with interest. "And is that the only thing —"

"I don't know you very well — yet."

Macheath gazed at her silently in the dimly flickering light of one lamp turned down low. His face was far from blank now. It glowed with pleasure and some suppressed excitement. "You wondered how you had met someone like me. The greater wonder is how I had the good fortune to meet you."

He put his hand inside his jacket and drew out the necklace. "I wish it were mine to give you, Marianne," he said, and dropped the puddle of diamonds into her hand. Dancing flames of purple and orange and green sparkled softly in the dim light.

"That you return them is gift enough, John. Thank you."

She returned his gaze, then on an impulse, stood on her tiptoes and placed a chaste kiss on his cheek. His arms closed around her and held on to her as if he would never let her go. He didn't kiss her, but she felt his cheek clinging to hers. Warm lips pressed on her hair and moved in a grazing motion to her forehead, her eyes. She held her breath, waiting for the coming assault on her lips.

He released her and said, in a businesslike voice, "I must go now. Be sure you lock the door behind me."

She was aware of a sharp sense of disappointment. "Very well."

"Don't be angry with me, love. I would be quite as persistent as Dirty Dick if I got started."

Marianne laughed and shook her head at the ludicrous comparison. She followed him to the door. He stopped and placed a fleeting kiss on her lips. "It is *au revoir*, not goodbye. I shall see you again soon, Marianne."

"Where? How? Oh, John, can't you tell me who you are?"

"You'll have to marry me to find that out, Miss Harkness."

"I couldn't marry a perfect stranger."

"In that case, I shall pay my respects to the duchess in the morning."

"You're not going out to rob another carriage?"

"Oh, ye of little faith! This is my night to return stolen goods." He withdrew the bag of jingling gold he had taken from McGinty. Then he was gone. She carefully locked the door and looked at the diamonds, wondering where she should put them for safe-keeping. She decided to put them on the duchess's night table.

If she awoke in the night, she would see them, along with the milk. And if, as was more likely, she slept until morning, they would be waiting for her as soon as she opened her eyes.

Marianne placed the diamonds on the night table and went to bed, smiling to think how happy her mistress would be and how that would improve her opinion of John. Her thoughts were all pleasant as she lay in bed, thinking of the future. John was coming in the morning. He would tell them who he was then. Who could he be? Fatigued from her busy night, she was soon sleeping soundly.

The duchess slept until eight-thirty that morning. Marianne awoke at eight and lay waiting for the shriek of joy. When she heard the duchess stirring, she crept quietly out of bed and went to peek in at her. She was sipping the milk and scowling at a bruise on her wrist, acquired during her rescue from the river.

"Oh, there you are, awake at last," the duchess said in her usual brusque way. "You took so long last night I fell asleep without my milk. It is stone cold now, with a scum on top of it. Come and help me up, Marianne. I ache in every joint after that mauling I suffered yesterday being hauled out of my rig."

Marianne looked at the duchess. She looked at the table, at the floor, the counterpane, and went dashing to the bedside.

"Where are they?" she asked.

"Where are what? What are you talking about, child?"

"The diamonds! I put them on your bedside table last night."

"My diamonds? Nonsense. You were dreaming. I had a vivid dream myself. I dreamed someone was trying to drown me in a vat of sour milk."

"No, no! I put the diamonds on your table last night to surprise you when you awoke this morning."

"Where are they, then?"

They both began scrabbling about the blankets, looking on the floor and under the bed.

"They're gone!" Marianne said in a voice of disbelief.

"How did you come by them?"

Marianne told the tale of her night's adventure. The duchess clamped her lips into a grim line and said, "I see how it is now. Macheath conned you, my girl. And he thinks to con me, but he has another think coming. And after I perjured myself to save his worthless neck from the gallows. He came creeping back and stole them again last night, trying to place the blame on someone else. And I, like a very greenhead, have told Bow Street he is my nephew. He counts on that to keep me quiet, you see, to protect the family name."

"No, it wasn't Macheath. He didn't know I would leave them on your table."

"He would have a pretty good idea where to look when he didn't find them in your room."

"He wasn't in my room. I locked my door."

"Has the lock been tampered with?"

"I don't know."

She ran back to her room but could find no sign of a forced entry. While she was gone, the duchess hauled herself out of bed and examined her own door. She saw a fresh scratch around the lock. Even more damning, the door was slightly ajar. Not actually open, but not properly closed, either. When she tried to close it, it would not stay shut. The mechanism had been broken.

"That proves nothing," she said, when Marianne joined her and saw the broken lock. "It only proves the bounder came in by my door rather than yours. The diamonds are the first thing he would see, sitting right there beneath the lamp. Foolish place to leave them. But then what can you expect from a simple girl like you? The lamp was burning low, you recall, though the oil has all been used up now. It must have been Macheath. Who else could it have been? I trust there is not more than one highwayman using this inn."

"All the highwaymen hereabouts use it," Marianne said in a dull, defeated voice. "And I even told Dirty Dick you are a duchess."

"Dirty Dick? What sort of name is that? What are you doing with such creatures?"

"That is the man who attacked me in the kitchen!"

"Really, Marianne. You must be more discriminating in the choice of men who attack you. Dirty Dick! What will folks say? At least Macheath is clean."

She perched on the edge of her bed and sat thinking, a scheming expression on her raddled old face. She looked up and said, "Yes, it might very well have been this Dirty Dick person, as you foolishly told him I was staying here. He would expect a duchess to be traveling with a chest of jewelry. It is all Macheath's fault for bringing us here, and he must rescue us. There is the villain who will get my diamonds back for me. Set a thief to catch a thief. Send for Macheath at once."

"He left last night, but he planned to return this morning to see you."

"Excellent! Ring for water. I must make a fresh toilette. And have breakfast. I am ravenous. Gammon and eggs — boiled, mind, not fried. And tell them to put a new lock on my door."

As she spoke, she gave the bell cord a yank herself and hobbled to her trunk to select a gown to entertain Macheath. She had not so enjoyed herself in years. She would have young Macheath leaping through hoops for her. What she really required was an escort to London, and if Macheath knew what was good for him, he would oblige her. How the old quizzes would stare to see her drive up with a handsome young flirt by her side.

Marianne, having convinced the duchess that Macheath had not stolen her diamonds, had now to convince herself. She had only his word for it that the other men here at the inn were highwaymen. He might have told her that to spread the blame when the diamonds disappeared. He might even have slipped a sleeping draft into her milk. It was odd she had slept through the robbery, for she was not a particularly heavy sleeper. And now that Bow Street thought he was the duchess's nephew, they would not suspect him.

But then there was Dirty Dick. He hadn't believed she was traveling with a duchess, but the clerk might have told him it was true. Macheath had taken the blunt Dirty Dick had stolen from some traveler. If Dick were in need of funds, he might have decided to try his hand at robbing the duchess. Yes, it might very well be Dirty Dick.

Her hopes were on Macheath's visit to see the duchess that morning, as he had promised. It might have been a ruse to get away without raising suspicion. He could be in London by now with the diamonds in his pocket, vanished forever in that city of over a million souls. Bow Street would never find him. But then why did he give back the diamonds if he only planned to run away? He would come. He must come.

CHAPTER
THIRTEEN

The two hours until Macheath arrived seemed like two years. A dozen times the flame of Marianne's faith wavered. He had intended to reform but found it beyond him — he was too deeply sunk in vice. He had changed his mind, stolen the necklace again, and left for good. No, John would not do that to her. She remembered that eager, innocent, boyish smile at the doorway when he told her he would speak to the duchess that very minute. She remembered his lips pressing on her forehead and the soft words he had spoken about his good fortune in finding her. Surely that had not been mere playacting?

But then there was that pistol he had pointed at Dirty Dick. He would have shot the man, had she not stopped him. He was a trained killer. The sort of brutish ferocity he had seen in Spain would be enough to degrade a saint. Her mood was in its dark mode when the long-awaited knock came at the duchess's door.

"Let him in," Her Grace said, arranging her best shawl about her shoulders.

Macheath came in smiling. "Your Grace, and Miss Harkness," he said, making an exquisite bow. He looked extremely elegant in an impeccably tailored jacket of blue superfine, a striped waistcoat, and fawn buckskins.

"I have come to beg your forgiveness, ma'am, and promise to mend my ways."

"I might forgive you yet, if you return my diamonds," she said with a glinting smile.

Macheath blinked, turned to Marianne, and said, "Ah, you have decided to allow me the pleasure of returning the necklace."

"It's gone, Macheath," Marianne said, and watched him like a spy, to read by his expression whether he was involved. He certainly looked thunderstruck by her words.

"Gone? What do you mean? What did you do with it?"

"I put it on the duchess's bedside table last night. It was gone when she awoke this morning. Her door had been pried open."

"What does Rooney say?"

"Who is Rooney?" the duchess asked.

"Why, the proprietor. Did you not tell him?"

"We were afraid it might be you," Marianne said.

A deep scowl seized his face. "Why would I have given it back if I meant to steal it again?"

"That is for you to tell us, Master Jackanapes," the duchess declared. She didn't really believe he had taken it, but she hoped that by casting doubts on him, he would feel obliged to prove his innocence by recovering the necklace.

"There scarcely seems any advantage to reforming, if my reputation is to follow me in this way," he said. "You didn't consider that the place is overrun with thieves? Any one of them might have pocketed the necklace. And you didn't even bother reporting it to Rooney or the constable."

"I believe in giving a thief a chance to reform, as you have good reason to know, sir," the duchess said. "If you did not take it yourself, Macheath, then I have no doubt you know or can discover which of your henchmen did the deed."

"I'll find it, never fear," he said grimly. "You can go on to London or stay here, just as you like. In fact, it will be easier if I don't have to worry about you two."

"Don't concern yourself with us," the duchess replied. "Just find my necklace. We can look after ourselves."

"It looks like it!" he said and strode angrily from the room.

The duchess nodded her satisfaction. "That has set a fire under the young whelp. We'll see results soon, Marianne. It is not worth our while leaving."

She went to the door and peered out. "He is going downstairs," she said. "This would be an excellent time for us to search his room, on the chance that he has hidden the diamonds there. I don't think it likely, but it will be best just to make sure."

Marianne heard this with grave misgivings. She knew from experience that "us" in such a context as this meant herself. "I don't know which room is his," she said.

"It shouldn't be hard to find out. You may be sure every pretty maid in the place is familiar with it." She gave the bell cord a jerk.

When a maid came to the door, the duchess said, "Tea, if you please. Oh, and while you are here, which room is Macheath's? I want to call on him."

"He's in the Hawthorn room, ma'am, just down the corridor and around the corner on the left, but he's not there now. He asked to have his mount sent round for him."

"Thank you. And send a man up to fix this lock at once."

"Yes, ma'am."

As soon as the maid left, the duchess said, "You run along and break into Macheath's room. Give it a good search mind. I would like to know who he really is. I have a feeling I've seen that nose before, and that bold, dark eye."

"Fitz-Matthew, you thought," Marianne reminded her.

"No, that's not it, though it is something like. Fitz-Matthew was never in the army. I believe Macheath was. He has a military walk and that short hair. His dark complexion, too, could have been picked up in Spain."

"He was in the army. He mentioned it."

"Did he? I don't recall that. Dragoons or infantry?"

"I don't know."

"See if you can find any personal papers. He might have kept his discharge. Hurry on now, before he comes back."

"How can I get into his room? They won't give me his key without his permission."

"Use your wits, girl. You have a hairpin, haven't you?"

Marianne went down the corridor, around the corner to the room with a hawthorn branch on the door. The door was locked, of course. Her hairpin proved ineffective. All she accomplished was to twist it out of shape. She remembered that at the duchess's mansion in Bath, one key fit all the bedroom doors. When she tried her own key in the lock, it was loose. She jiggled it about for a minute and found that by pressing the key to the right, the lock opened. She stepped into the room and closed the door quietly behind her.

It was like stepping into a barracks. The room was spartan, everything neat as a pin. That might be Miguel's work. She surveyed the room, then went to the clothespress and began to search the pockets of the three jackets hanging there. She found a little loose change, a fishhook, a comb, and a few IOUs, but no diamonds and no identification. She continued searching, shaking out the boots and slippers, then on to the toilet table with its handsome array of brushes, shaving equipment, and a few modest cravat pins in a leather box. She drew open the drawers and fumbled quickly through the linens and small cloths, all without success.

The bed was next — under the pillows, under the mattress, under the bed itself. It had no canopy, so she didn't have to climb up on a chair and examine the top. The last remaining place was the desk, and its surface

120

held only a few sheets of writing paper, a blotting pad, a recent copy of the *Morning Observer*, an ink pot, and a pen. None of the blottings on the pad were legible. She opened the top drawer and saw a set of news clippings held together by a pin. She rifled through them. They dealt with various highway robberies, perhaps his own. A thousand pounds stolen from an M.P., a watch, and an emerald ring from his wife. One hundred guineas reward for his capture. Her heart thudded heavily.

There were others, many others. The victims were all notable, all connected either with government or the supplying of arms and goods to Spain. These would be the people Macheath had railed against getting fat while the veterans had to beg for a crumb. They were eminent enough men that the price on Macheath's head rose from one hundred guineas to five hundred and then to a thousand. If the duchess knew that, she would turn him in in a minute.

She scanned them quickly and began rifling other drawers, looking for the diamonds. But in her heart she no longer believed Macheath had them. He was a good thief, insofar as intentions went. She found nothing to indicate his name. Other than the clippings and his clothes, the room was impersonal. It might have been hired as a temporary pied-à-terre by any gentleman of fashion.

She turned to leave. That was when she heard a soft footfall outside the door. It was probably only a servant or some other guest going to his room, but her heart beat faster. Then the steps stopped at the door, and her heart leapt into her throat. The knob turned silently. There was no tap at the door, as a servant would make. Who could it be?

The door did not open immediately. She stared, transfixed, looking about for some place to hide. With only a split second to think, she picked up the clothes brush from his toilet table and ran toward the door. She was concealed behind it as it opened. The first thing she saw was a hand holding a pistol. That was enough to throw her into a spasm of alarm. The next thing was the back of a man's head with a curled beaver on it. Acting on instinct, she raised her hand and struck his head with the brush as hard as she could, planning to dart out the door when he fell to the ground.

Unfortunately, the man's head was hard. The blow didn't knock him unconscious, or even off his stride. It only knocked his hat off. He turned swiftly. The hand not holding a gun reached out and clamped on to her wrist. The brush fell to the floor as he swung her out where he could see her. She stared at the glittering eyes and hard-set jaw of Macheath in a fine fit of temper. He stared at her as if he'd never seen her before, as if she were just an enemy.

"The servant said you had left! I was just — just leaving you a note?" she said in a breathless rush, ending on a betraying, questioning tone.

"A billet-doux, no doubt," he sneered. When she didn't answer, he said, "Get out," in a hard, cold voice. The same voice that had demanded they "stand and deliver". He tossed the gun on the bed and stood, arms folded, waiting for her to leave.

"All right! I'm going, but you need not mount your high horse with me, Captain. How can you expect us to trust you, when you are an admitted thief?"

"I only stole diamonds. You have done worse." He unfolded his arms and took a step toward her. The anger had left his voice, but it was still in his eyes, and in the frown between them. He spoke in low tones. "Last night you protected me. You let me believe you trusted me. You have stolen my —" His lips clamped shut, as if he had to force himself to hold in the fateful words. Marianne knew what he had been about to say. She had stolen his heart. His angry, wounded expression said it as clearly as words.

"How can we trust you? You won't even tell us your name. That's really what I was looking for. We didn't think you had the diamonds."

"What's in a name?"

"You have a pat answer for everything," she said with a *tsk* of annoyance.

"No more. I'm all out of answers."

"You didn't find the necklace?"

"I was just having a word with McGinty." He rubbed the knuckles of his right hand, suggesting the words had been physical in nature. "He takes breakfast with his daughter, who lives in a cottage a mile down the road. I met him coming back, which is why I returned earlier than you expected. I am convinced he didn't take the diamonds himself, but I wager he told one of his colleagues the duchess was here."

"Have you any idea who?"

"I found out from Rooney who McGinty was drinking with after I relieved him of that bag of gold. I'm on my way to have a little chat with the fellow now."

"Thank you." Marianne stood a moment, wanting to apologize, or clear the air between them in some manner, but she had little experience in dealing with beaux. "I'm sorry I hit you. I hope I didn't hurt you." She waited for him to forgive her.

"I have a hard head, to match my heart," he said with a wave of his hand.

"I don't think you have a heart at all."

He cast a long, searching look at her. "All men have a heart, even we thieves. I have heard a rumor even some ladies have one."

As he was being sarcastic, she pouted and said, "I had best go now."

"She told you to come?"

"Yes."

"How did you get in? The lock isn't damaged."

"I used my own key. It fits the lock."

He just shook his head. "I might have known. In the future, when you smash someone's room, I suggest you determine first how long he will be away."

"Thank you. I'll bear that in mind."

"Are you going to London now?"

"Her Grace has every faith that you will find her necklace soon. She plans to wait and take it with her."

"Is she as horrible to live with as I think?"

"I am all out of answers, too. I'm sorry, John." His mood softened as she spoke his name. "About — you

124

know, sneaking into your room when you weren't here, hitting you."

"It would have been more enjoyable had you come last night when I *was* here. No need to tell Her Grace that our keys open each other's door, eh?"

She frowned as she considered the implications of this. Her fingers flew to her lips. "Oh!"

"A wasted opportunity. Ah well, let us hope there will be more opportunities in the future. And now, before you have a heart attack, I shall let you go."

"I am one of those ladies who has a heart, am I?" she asked saucily.

"A hard one, like my head."

"How hard it is won't make any difference to Jack Ketch, though, will it? One thousand pounds reward . . ."

"So you have been reading my clippings. They have to catch me first."

"If the duchess had known that last night when Officer Bruce called on her, I doubt you would be here now."

"Will you tell her?"

"Of course not!"

"You want the reward for yourself?" he asked, smiling to show he trusted her.

"I'll wait until it goes up to two thousand."

"It has," he said. "Ancaster wields a big stick."

"Oh, John!"

"Don't worry, Marianne. I'm through with all that. You have convinced me my life is worth more than a couple of thousand pounds."

He held the door, chewing back a smile as she dashed out, peering over her shoulder to look back at him. She flew around the corner and to her own room. By the time she reached it, her frown had changed to a wary smile. She tried to remember at what point he had stopped being angry. It was when he had asked if the duchess made her go to his room. He had indicated before that he pitied her. Was that why he was sometimes friendly with her, because he pitied her? She didn't want pity. But she did want John Macheath, and she wanted him before one of his "friends" turned him in for the reward.

CHAPTER
FOURTEEN

It was late afternoon before Marianne saw Captain Macheath again. The duchess had become restless as the afternoon wore on and he still had not come. She had a few moments' pleasure ragging at the locksmith who came to fix her lock, but other than that, her complaints were all about the captain.

"You are sure he knows who the scoundrel is who has my diamonds?" she asked half a dozen times.

"He said he got a name from Rooney."

"I hope nothing has happened to him," the duchess said, causing a new worry. "We would only deceive ourselves to think all the highwaymen are as civil as our captain," she informed Marianne. That "our" had a very possessive sound to it. "Most of them would as lief put a bullet through their victim as not. We may count ourselves very fortunate to have been held up by an officer and a gentleman."

This confirmed that the duchess had succumbed to a new flirt. She was not exactly a laughingstock among her friends, but it was known that if she took a fancy to a handsome face, its possessor would soon find himself the object of her generosity, whether he wanted it or not. This generosity did not extend to financial help, however. It would take more than good looks to pry money out of her. Her assistance was confined to helping him make the proper connections, to finding a good position or a good wife. She was not at all lecherous. Marianne had long ago figured out these "beaux" were surrogate sons. The duchess had no sons. She had three daughters, all married long since and settled into motherhood — and in some cases, grandmotherhood.

"How dark it is, for the middle of the afternoon. We shan't get away today, Marianne. We must make an early start tomorrow. That will still allow us one day to rest before the wedding. I shan't deprive you of your tour of London. We shall stay a few days after the wedding before going on to Levenhurst with Eugenie."

Eugenie was her eldest daughter, who made her home in Hertford, north of London. The duchess was to visit her for a week before returning to Bath. Eugenie's husband was a Methodist. It was known that he conducted a prayer service for his household three times a day, did not believe in drink, and, if forced to dance, danced on only one leg. Marianne was not much looking forward to the visit, nor was the duchess for that matter.

"Let us order dinner. It will help pass the time," the dame said a little later.

Dinner was ordered and soon arrived. The joint was condemned for toughness and the potatoes and peas for mushiness but both were consumed, along with a bottle of wine. Her Grace was just drawing out her cards when the tap came at the door. Macheath

128

entered, looking hagged and somewhat battered, and still wearing his afternoon clothes.

"A gentleman usually changes into evening clothes after the sun sets, Macheath," the duchess said. Fascination with a gentleman never had the effect of lowering her social standards.

"I thought you would want to know about your diamonds as soon as possible, Your Grace," he replied. Marianne knew he had not recovered them. When he turned his glance to her, there was no sparkle in his eyes, no mischievous grin. But as the glance lengthened to a gaze, his expression did soften to something like pleasure.

"Well, where are they?" Her Grace demanded. "Hand them over."

"I don't have them."

The noble spine stiffened. A haughty sneer settled on the duchess's aged countenance. "I see. You have chosen to throw your lot in with the other thieves. Just what one might expect. Send for the constable, Marianne."

"Yes, do — if you never want to see the necklace again," Macheath said, unfazed.

The duchess squinted her rheumy eyes at him. "What does that mean, if anything?"

"I have instituted a plan to recover it. McGinty has a fellow he works with, his name's La Rue. He is the brains of the pair. Mind you, La Rue is no genius, either. I am convinced he has the necklace. I've searched his cottage. It's not there, nor is he. He's run to ground. The fence from London will be here on the weekend. It saves us taking our wares to London," he explained. "That's when La Rue will hand over the sparklers for a quarter or less of their worth."

"But they're worth five thousand! You can't expect me to pay a quarter of their value to get back my own necklace."

"That is not what I'm suggesting."

"If you mean to steal them when the fence comes, it will be too late," the duchess said. "I want them for the wedding. I want them now."

"That was my first plan. I have another one, if you aren't willing to wait. Unfortunately, there might be a little danger in it for you."

"I care nothing for that. Let us hear it."

"La Rue got your diamonds. They were sitting in plain sight." The duchess glared at Marianne. "Seeing such a treasure, he may have just grabbed them and run. The room did not appear to have been searched. We might convince him you are carrying other valuables. If we could lure him back again, I would be waiting in your room to catch him. Then we threaten to call Bow Street if he doesn't return the diamonds. He'll agree to it."

The duchess didn't hesitate a minute. "Done!" she said. "And Marianne and I will be here to help you."

"That will not be necessary, Your Grace. I can handle La Rue. When I said you might be in danger, I meant you would be next door, possibly exposed to some minimal risk due to a flying bullet. Though actually there is no reason you must remain in that room. You could use mine."

"I'm sure you are as brave as a pride of lions, Macheath, but even a trained soldier might be overborne by chance. You will certainly require some backup. We shall be right here, in this room, to give a hand if necessary."

"Miguel can help me."

"You are very anxious to be alone with La Rue and my diamonds," she said, instantly suspicious. "I only know what you choose to tell me. For all I know, you may have recovered my necklace already and are now devising this scheme to lay the blame on La Rue. What is to prevent you from shooting him and going off scot-free with my diamonds?"

His face stiffened in fury. His nostrils flared and his eyes glittered dangerously. He took two deep breaths to rein his temper before replying. "I am flattered at your assessment of my character, ma'am. If you wish to be here and risk dying of heart attack, then by all means stay."

"I shall," she said. "Are you sure you can trust this Rooney fellow? He sounds like an Irishman."

"He is. What of it?" She did not reply to this taunt. "Rooney has helped me out in a spot before. He'll see La Rue gets the word you are traveling with other valuables. He has no fondness for La Rue."

"La Rue might smell a trap," the duchess objected. "You have called on me half a dozen times. He knows you and I are friends."

"Then he knows more than I do!"

"He knows there is some association between us, was my meaning. Odd you should buck at a chance for friendship with a duchess. No doubt you would be happier if I were a light-skirt."

Macheath's lips twitched in amusement. "We have different ideas of friendship, Your Grace. As to La Rue suspecting I am involved, I shall make a showy departure for London before nightfall and slip back into the inn after dark to join you here. I would prefer to wait until the fence comes, but as you are so eager —"

"We'll do it tonight. Now run along and get the plan started."

"I am on my way." He cast a resigned glance at Marianne and bowed to the ladies.

"The captain should eat first. He must be hungry, Your Grace," Marianne said.

"Aye, and dirty as well. A gentleman never calls on a lady in such a disgusting state. Wash up before you eat, mind. And don't keep us up too late, Captain. We are leaving early in the morning. You will accompany us to London, of course, to prevent any further disasters."

Macheath stared at her in disbelief. "I have other plans for tomorrow."

"How are we to make sure the diamonds are safe, if we don't have an escort?"

"You should have thought of that before you left Bath."

"Well, upon my word! There is gratitude for you. When I perjured myself to Officer Bruce, Captain, it was understood you would see me safely to Grosvenor Square."

"It was not understood by me."

"It is up to you. It is not too late to report the matter now. Your posing as my nephew will not deter me. I had not seen Fitz-Matthew for aeons. I did not recognize at first that you were an impostor. Run down and ask Rooney to send the constable around, Marianne."

Marianne peered up at Macheath. The look they exchanged was not far from conspiratorial. They both knew the duchess was bluffing. His angry brow softened. "Perhaps if you ask me very nicely, I shall accompany you to London, Your Grace," he said, but it was at Marianne that he gazed.

The duchess reached out and jiggled his arm until he looked at her. "I won't have you flirting with Marianne. She is a simple country gel who would only go imagining she is in love with you. And besides, she hasn't a penny of dowry. You shan't sit in our carriage. You must ride your mount along beside it. When the other thieves see we are accompanied by you, they will leave us alone. But keep your pistol charged, just in case."

"What time are we leaving?" he asked.

"Early. I want to be off at first light. We shall meet downstairs at eight-thirty. Hire us a private parlor. Now when we get to London, Macheath, I want you to call on Lord Philmont, at Whitehall. He is my nephew. I shall give you a letter of introduction and a character reference. He will put you on to some honest work. If you can keep your fingers out of other people's pockets, I daresay you will get on. You have a decent jacket, and some address. Presentable bachelors are always at a premium in London. With luck, you might even nab some undemanding cit's daughter with a few thousand dowry. I shall have a look about for one while I am there."

"You are too kind, ma'am," he said, in a voice that suggested she was an interfering old fool.

"That is quite all right," she said, unoffended. It was beyond her comprehension that anyone could make fun of her. She was the Duchess of Bixley.

"I won't have you carrying on with low company after you are married. Serving wenches won't do your career any good. Do you have any politics at all? No, I thought not," she said, before he could reply. "You are a Tory. The Tories have all the perquisites these days, since Prinny has changed his coat."

"I am a Whig," he said. He bowed, winked at Marianne, and left.

"Come right back and tell us what La Rue says!" Her Grace hollered after him. When he was gone, she turned to Marianne. "I like a spunky fellow. He will do fine with Philmont. I shouldn't be surprised to see him made a minister of something-or-other before he is through, if they don't hang him first. Of course we will have to find him a seat in Parliament. Eugenie's husband has a couple in his giving. Get my brush, Marianne. My hair is all tumbling about my ears. You might want to do something to your own toilette as well. And wipe that smirk off your face. You look like a simpleton."

Marianne removed the duchess's cap and arranged her coiffure before going to her own room. She closed the door behind her, to allow privacy. She had been with the duchess all day and felt the need of solitude. Her mirror told her she was "in looks." The glow in her eyes and the flush on her cheeks were becoming to her. She didn't think Macheath thought she looked like a simpleton.

How wonderful it would be if the duchess really could reclaim him and find him a position in London. London! Would she be living there one day? After he was established, would Macheath come and claim her? "You have stolen my heart." That was what he was going to say, but pride prevented him. And he had stolen hers.

She tidied her hair and picked up her manicure scissors to cut a fingernail that had cracked during her scramble out of the carriage yesterday and had been catching on her clothes. The one shorter nail ruined the symmetry of her hands. She took up a nail file to smooth the rough edges.

She was interrupted by a light tap at the door and slid the file into her pocket. She opened the door to find Macheath in the corridor. "Are you alone?" he asked in a low voice.

"Yes. Come in."

He entered and began pacing the small room. "I am a little concerned about the duchess's heart," he said. "Do you think it is up to the excitement of the plan I suggested? She is old, frail. I never intended for her to be in the same room with La Rue."

"I am concerned," she said at once. "I'll try to talk her into staying in this room."

"With the door bolted."

"No, she won't stand for that. She doesn't really suspect you of those horrid things she said, you know. She just likes annoying people and knowing what is going on. She will be poking her head in to see what is happening every minute. Unless . . ." She looked at him, reluctant to say what she had in mind. It seemed a betrayal of her mistress's trust to suggest it.

"Right. I'll order her a bottle of brandy. Make sure she doesn't make herself sick with it again. With luck, she'll doze off before La Rue comes."

"That was what I had in mind," she admitted, rather sheepishly.

"How do you put up with the harridan? I had thought Spain was bad. It was a holiday compared to being with her."

"Why do *you* stay with her? You have had a dozen chances to leave."

He gave her a gently chiding look that sent the blood pounding through her veins. "Why do you think I stay, Marianne?" he asked softly and took her two hands in his.

"You — you had better go, John."

"I'm on my way, love." He placed a fleeting kiss on her lips and walked quickly out the door.

Marianne stood motionless a moment, enjoying the tingle on her lips and the joyful glow that engulfed her.

CHAPTER
FIFTEEN

At eleven o'clock, Macheath returned to the duchess's room. Marianne had joined her some time before and was reading the journal aloud to her mistress.

"What kept you so long?" the impatient duchess demanded.

"You forget I had to bathe, change, eat dinner, let it be known in the taproom I was leaving for London, leave, and return circuitously on foot to slip up the backstairs. All things considered, I think I made excellent time. La Rue is playing cards belowstairs. He won't come before two or three in the morning."

"I have been thinking it's a pity I had the lock repaired. Will he be able to get in, do you think?"

Macheath looked at it, drew a small metal tool from his pocket, stuck it in the lock, and turned it with no difficulty. "I wouldn't worry about it, Your Grace."

"What is your Miguel up to? Keeping an eye on La Rue, is he?"

"He's playing cards with him."

"Odd name for an Englishman, Miguel."

"He is not English. He's Irish. A Spanish woman gave him the name."

"A light-skirt, I wager. He was wise not to marry a foreigner. I have no opinion of foreigners."

"Unusual, Your Grace," he said blandly. "You usually have an opinion on everything."

As the duchess did not offer him a seat, he found himself a chair and sat down. Behind the duchess's back, Marianne held up the unopened bottle of brandy Macheath had sent up. Her Grace hadn't touched a drop of it. She wanted to be wide awake for whatever transpired later.

"Why don't we play a few hands of cards to pass the time?" Marianne suggested. She knew her mistress liked to have a glass by her when she played cards. She would not allow herself to become inebriated, but it would get the bottle open at least, and when the game was over, she would likely keep sipping.

"A pity we hadn't a fourth and we could play whist," the dame said. Whist was her game of choice, but she was no stranger to *vingt-et-un* or even, when she was reduced to playing with her servants, Pope Joan or All-Fours. They settled for *vingt-et-un*, to be played at the desk with the duchess in the one comfortable chair and the others with their legs twisted at an awkward angle at the sides of the desk.

"Would anyone like something to drink before we begin?" Marianne asked.

"That brandy looks tempting," Macheath replied promptly.

"No brandy, Captain," the duchess said. "We must keep our wits about us."

"I have a hard head, ma'am. We drank a little more than usual in the Peninsula, you must know. I can handle it."

"An army man, eh? I thought as much. Dragoons or infantry?"

"Cavalry, Sixth Division."

Her interest in this was to determine whether he could afford a horse when he entered the army. The better class of man was in the cavalry.

"A sergeant?" she ventured.

"A colonel, actually."

"Promoted on the field of battle, eh? It is an excellent way for a penniless fellow to get ahead in the world. That won't do you any harm when you are looking for a post in London."

As they spoke, Marianne poured the amber liquid slowly into his glass at the table, watching as the duchess eyed it covetously.

"Perhaps just a wee tot for me, well watered," she said finally. "My throat is dry, here by the grate."

Marianne poured her a tot and let the duchess water it herself. Marianne drank water flavored with a few drops of brandy.

As the game proceeded, Macheath poured himself another glass and offered the bottle to the duchess. She complained of the weakness of her brew and fortified it with another splash of brandy. Macheath and Marianne made sure she enjoyed a winning streak, to lessen her fears of losing a few pennies at the game.

By midnight, she was becoming querulous that La Rue had not come. "Doesn't he realize I must be up early in the morning? It is very thoughtless of him to wait so long to come to steal my jewels."

"He may be waiting until the lights are out. He wouldn't come while you are up and awake," Marianne said.

"Of course! What a set of ninnyhammers we are! He may have been listening at the door for all we know, and here we have been gabbling like tinkers. Douse the lamps at once, Marianne."

"I really don't think he will be here for a few hours yet," Macheath said.

"Devil take him. I need my sleep. I shall have a little lie-down in your room, Marianne. You come with me. Macheath can wait here in the dark. We don't want La Rue to hear any voices when he comes. That is nine pence you owe me, Macheath, and you owe me thruppence, Marianne. I shall take it off your next quarter's wages. I wouldn't want to leave you short of funds in London."

Macheath handed her her winnings, which she put into her reticule with satisfaction. He felt a stab of pity for Marianne, to think three pence could be considered a sum worth worrying about. The duchess bustled Marianne into the other room. Her Grace lay on the bed, fully dressed.

"Leave the door open a few inches so that we shall hear if Macheath needs our help," she said. "You might just have the poker handy. I'll let you wield it. My shoulder is acting up since my dunking in the river."

140

"We should extinguish the lamp in this room as well, Your Grace. That will make it look as if no one is awake here, either."

"Yes, go ahead, but mind you don't fall asleep. Wake me the minute you hear La Rue. I want to get a look at the scoundrel."

"Very well. I'll just sit here by the grate where there is a bit of light."

They settled in for the vigil. The duchess was not inebriated, but she was thoroughly relaxed and after half an hour, Marianne heard those snuffling sounds that indicated her mistress would soon be snoring. When the snores became loud and regular, she tip-toed to the adjoining door. Across the room she saw Macheath. He had placed a blanket and some pillows on the floor and lay by the grate with his chin propped on his palms, staring into the fire. The leaping flames cast flickering shadows over his face. He looked pensive. Not worried, exactly, but not easy in his mind, either. When she went forward, he rose and offered her his hand.

"She's sleeping," Marianne said softly.

"So I hear. She sounds like a grampus. Sit here by the fire. Do you want a blanket for your shoulders?"

"My shawl will do," she said, sitting beside him. When he arranged her shawl, he left his arm over her shoulder. "Have you heard anything yet?" she said, pretending not to notice.

"No. It's still early. When we hear him fiddling with the doorknob, I want you to run into the other room and close the door."

"My mistress wants me to leave it open."

He looked at her with a quizzing grin. "What a good little girl. Do you always do what you're told?"

"I am not so biddable as that. Only when it is my employer who speaks. Are you really going to accompany us to London, or did you just pretend to conciliate her?"

"I'm a man of my word."

"You obey, when the alternative is a brush with the law, you mean."

"That is not why I agreed to go." He reached out and folded her fingers in his warm hand. "You know why I am going. I have been feeling for some time that I have been on the scamp lay long enough. If I found some position at Whitehall, I might do more good than I can on my own. Do something to help all the veterans, I mean, not just the few I can give my ill-got gains to."

"I'm happy to hear it, John. What you do is too dangerous."

"Very true. One never knows when he will run up against a tyrant like the duchess." He smiled softly, with affection glowing in his dark eyes. When he spoke again, she heard a serious note in his voice she hadn't heard before. "Since meeting you, I realize the need of a more settled life. I cannot ask you to marry me yet, but one day . . ."

It was the most commitment Marianne could expect from a man in his position, and she was more than satisfied with it. As she studied Macheath's face, bathed in darting light and shadows, she knew she would wait as long as it took, forever if necessary. She had set out on this journey hoping to meet some dull provincial gentleman in need of a wife, and she had found her dream lover. A handsome, dashing hero, even if he was an outlaw.

"How long do you remain in London?" he asked.

"A week, then a week in Hertford, and a few stops on the way back to Bath. It is so far away," she said, sighing to think of Macheath in London, on the other side of the country.

The duchess's snores were a counterpoint to their conversation. Between fearing she would wake up and listening for La Rue to come, they were on edge. They sat together before the dancing flames, listening for a sound as they gazed at the fire and each other.

"You look like a devil, with the fire reflected in your eyes," she said.

"You look like an angel. An angel with her hair on fire." His fingers twined lovingly in her tresses, which caught the firelight and reflected it.

"I'm glad you'll be staying in London," she said. "La Rue or McGinty or someone might turn you in if you stayed here."

"No highwayman would turn in a fellow scamp. His life wouldn't be worth a brass farthing. The other scamps would take care of him. It's an unwritten law. Would it bother you if I was turned in?"

She looked up to see him staring down at her. "You know it would." Then she gave him a pert smile. "'A simple country gel' like me."

"You left out the best part. 'Imagining she is in love.' Are you imagining it, I wonder? Bowled over by my reckless derring-do?"

"I never said I was in love."

He tilted her chin up and pressed his mouth to hers. "You said it," he told her, with smug satisfaction, then he kissed her hard on the lips, to prove it to himself. The blood quickened in his veins as she responded to his ardor.

He was suddenly seized with a reckless impatience to get on with the night's work.

"I'm going to run down and ask Rooney to see what is afoot in the card parlor. I hope La Rue hasn't drunk himself into a stupor."

"Oh dear. Do you think he might have?"

"It's possible. Don't worry about it. If he has, I'll see Rooney sobers him up before dawn. I'll be right back. Don't let anyone in but me."

"Of course."

He rose and went out the door, warning Marianne to lock it behind him. She tiptoed into the next room to see that the duchess was comfortable. She snored on, oblivious to the world.

CHAPTER
SIXTEEN

When the light tap came at Marianne's door a little later, she assumed it was Macheath and went running to answer it. Even when she saw the black mask and the pistol, she thought it was Macheath. He was wearing his mask so he would not be recognized, as he was supposed to be in London, and was carrying his pistol for defense. The other masked man behind him would be Miguel. But as she looked more closely, she realized the larger man was not Macheath.

He had not been wearing soiled buckskins and a rough jacket. The hand holding the pistol was not his well-manicured hand. These details flashed through her mind in a second. That was enough time for the intruders to get a foot in the door and overpower her. Just as she opened her lips to shout, one of them clamped a rough hand over her mouth. The other yanked her arms behind her back and tied them together.

By the time the gag had been stuffed in her mouth and the blanket thrown over her head, she was fairly certain the men were La Rue and a cohort — likely McGinty.

She flailed and kicked and tried to spit out the dirty rag. All was in vain. The gag was not only stuffed into her mouth but tied behind her head. One of the men held her tight. They spoke in whispers, their voices muffled by their masks. She heard the words "blunt" and "jewelry," and so they *had* come looking for what else they could steal from the duchess. She heard one of them moving about the room quietly, opening drawers, rifling the duchess's belongings. The other held her immobile. Then she heard the awful words, "We'll take the chit. She'll do as well — better. We'll hold her to ransom."

"Aye," the smaller man said in leering accents that she recognized as McGinty's. "Macheath'll pay handsome for the wench."

The larger man lifted her into his arms without speaking another word and carried her through the corridor, down a flight of stairs, out into the chilly night air.

When Macheath went downstairs, Rooney told him no one had left the card parlor. Macheath wasn't surprised. He was sure La Rue and McGinty would wait until two or three o'clock before paying their visit to the duchess's room. He had time to have a look around outside. Nothing unusual was going forth there, either. He went to the stable to see what mount La Rue was riding that night. He had two: a black stallion he used for robbing coaches and a bay mare he rode at other times.

The bay mare was in one stall, McGinty's cob in another, so they were still at the card table.

"Looks like La Rue ain't planning a job tonight," the ostler said with a knowing grin.

Macheath checked out the duchess's team while he was there, and had a word with her groom to see if the carriage was fit to travel. Over the days, he had achieved respect, if not quite friendship, from the servants.

"Her Grace wants to continue on to London in the morning. She plans to leave around nine."

"I'll be ready and waiting," Beeton assured him.

As Macheath headed back to the inn, he began to wonder about those mounts in the stable. La Rue and McGinty would want to make a fast getaway. They'd go down the backstairs after the robbery. If they went out that little side door that led to the brewhouse, the most convenient place to tether their nags would be the mulberry tree behind the house. It would be more private as well. Were the mounts in the stable a red herring? Did they have other horses waiting behind the brewhouse? He decided to have a look.

His route took him past the window of the card parlor. He ducked down to avoid being seen as he passed. He looked behind the brewhouse and saw the nags were there — Diablo and a pigeon-gray mare he recognized as belonging to a friend of McGinty's. McGinty rode it from time to time.

When he returned, he was surprised to notice the window of the card parlor was open. La Rue liked his cigar, but on a chilly night like this . . . Macheath went forward and crouched below the window, hoping to overhear their conversation. There wasn't a sound from within. It must be a tense game. He waited, and when the silence continued for sixty seconds, he lifted his head and peeked inside. At first glance, the room looked empty. There were no shoulders bent over the table. Had they decided to play somewhere else? Odd Rooney hadn't mentioned it.

He took a closer look — and saw the cards strewn over the board. There was someone in one of the chairs, dead drunk, with his head resting on the wood. Miguel! Impossible. Miguel could outdrink a camel. His drink had certainly been doctored to render him unconscious. Macheath clambered in the window and ran to Miguel. Only drugged, not dead, thank God. The open window told him why Rooney had not alerted him. La Rue had slipped out the window to avoid being seen.

Macheath dashed out to have a word with Rooney. "They've gone out the window. Miguel's been drugged. Look after him for me, Rooney. Their mounts are still there. They must be abovestairs now."

"Shall I go up with you?"

"I can handle them. But how did they get past your desk to go upstairs? Did you leave it unattended?"

"That I did not!"

He tossed up his hands. "They didn't pass the desk, of course. They used the backstairs."

"Must have done. The game was still on a quarter of an hour ago. I took in a pitcher of ale. Your man looked fine then."

148

A small smile curved Macheath's lips. "I'll be down presently," he said, and drawing out his pistol, he headed for the stairs.

He took them two at a time, expecting to find La Rue rummaging around in the duchess's room. He was not very worried. They hadn't had time to hurt Marianne. He saw the door to the duchess's room hanging open. He tiptoed forward, every nerve stretched taut. And when he got there, he saw the room was empty. A glance told him La Rue had made a quick search. Drawers hung open, pillows were scattered on the floor. He noticed the adjoining door was closed, and the fierce pounding of his heart dulled to a thud.

He'd have to go after La Rue, but first he wanted to confirm that Marianne and the duchess were all right. Marianne must have scuttled into the next room and closed the door when she heard them coming. She was probably there now, cowering behind it, thinking the sounds she heard were La Rue, come back to terrify her.

He went to the door. "It's me, Marianne," he called softly. When the door didn't open, he drew it open and peered in. The duchess lay peacefully in her bed, but of Marianne there was no sign. He threw the door wide open and went in, heart pounding. He lit the lamp on the toilet table and turned it up to its full brightness to look all around. Marianne was gone. His heart was a block of ice in his chest. As if moving on strings, he went and looked into the clothespress, the only article in the room large enough to conceal a body. It held only gowns and pelisses. She was gone. La Rue had gotten her.

He stood a moment, paralyzed with fear, looking around in disbelief, unable to credit this had happened so quickly, that he had let it happen. Marianne at the mercy of those two thugs. He went to give the duchess a shake to rouse her, but stopped with his hand two inches above her shoulder. She looked so old, so pitifully frail.

He'd let her sleep on. What was the point of frightening the old girl? It would only bring on an attack. She had obviously slept through the whole thing, so she couldn't tell him what had happened.

He quelled the rising panic and tried to think. Fifteen minutes ago they had been at the card table. Two minutes ago their mounts were still behind the brewhouse. They must have heard him coming and hidden. He dashed back downstairs. Rooney came running out to meet him.

"They've gotten away with Marianne, Rooney. She's not in her room."

"They can't have gone far carrying a woman over their shoulders. Maybe they're still in the building. I'll search the inn."

"Thanks."

Macheath ran out to the brewhouse, to see the two mounts calmly chomping the grass. He tore back to the inn stable. Odd they'd use the public stable when they were encumbered with a hostage. Both La Rue's and McGinty's mounts were still there. It was impossible.

They hadn't gone on foot, carrying a struggling woman in their arms.

Oh God, they'd killed her. No, they wouldn't risk murder. They had taken her away, somehow. McGinty had a room here at the inn. She wouldn't likely be there either, but he had best look, just in case. He went out and hurried around the corner, down a corridor to the little room under the eaves that McGinty called home.

The door was locked. Macheath unceremoniously kicked it in and strode into the room, lit a lamp, and took a look around. McGinty wasn't there, nor could he find any clue as to where he might be. No convenient note, only a pile of IOUs he'd probably never collect. Perkins, Mallory, Simmons, Perkins again, for ten guineas. He tossed them aside and ran downstairs, out the front door. He wasn't fortunate enough to find anyone lingering outside the inn who would have seen them if they had taken the main road. They could have gone in any direction.

His mind automatically went into its military mode. He had a certain amount of territory to cover, and he couldn't do it alone. His best helper, his faithful batman Miguel, was *hors de* combat. He needed willing volunteers. Beeton and Tom were the obvious men. He hastened to the stable and informed them of what had happened.

"They didn't come this way. You figure they plan to hold her for ransom?" Beeton asked.

"So I assume."

"I wonder how much the old malkin would be willing to pay," he said doubtfully.

"I'll pay whatever they ask, if it comes to that."

"What can we do?"

"They haven't been gone long. We'll divide up the territory."

Macheath was familiar with every fence and hut and creek in the neighborhood. He sketched a hasty map, pinpointing possible destinations where they might have taken Marianne.

"We'll search La Rue's cottage, though I doubt he'd be foolish enough to take her there. There's an abandoned gristmill just here, on the riverbank. That's a possibility. And Simmons's cottage just here," he said, marking the spot with a star. "He's a friend of McGinty's, but a family man. Take a look, just in case." He tore off that portion of the map and gave it to Beeton. "You have a gun?"

Beeton patted his pocket. "I have."

"You, Tom?"

"The old fowling piece — you've seen it."

"Take it. It's better than nothing." He went over another section of the map with Tom.

"This'll take a while on foot," Tom said. "We don't have mounts. Just the team from the carriage."

"I'll speak to John Groom. They have nags for hire."

He had a hasty word with the ostler, who led two undistinguished jades from their loose boxes. Beeton and Tom were happy to get a leg over any piece of horseflesh. They didn't get much opportunity to ride in Bath. Much struck with the captain's expertise, they saluted before riding off on their mission, looking dreadfully like Don Quixote and Sancho Panza.

152

Macheath saved for himself what he considered the most likely place to find Marianne. But before leaving, he ran back into the inn.

"Any luck?" he asked Rooney. Rooney shook his head.

"The servants have searched the place. They're not here, Macheath. It just struck me — Jim Todd is at the inn tonight."

"He wouldn't be working with La Rue. He's a respectable farmer."

"He is, and a clutch-fisted one. He takes his little wagon and cob into the forest at night to save a few pence stable fees. If they were carrying Miss Harkness, they might have made free of it, eh?"

"I was heading into the forest in any case. I'll have a look."

He hurried outside, mounted his mare, and rode the few yards to the forest behind the inn. The night was crisp and cold. The afternoon clouds had blown off to reveal a jet-black sky sprinkled with diamond dust. A star-dogged fingernail of moon cast a wan light below. He had often seen Jim Todd's little wagon tied to a spreading elm in a clearing in the forest. It wasn't there. If La Rue was using it to transport Marianne, he would likely avoid the main road. People hereabouts knew Jim and his red wagon. They'd find it odd if La Rue was driving it.

He led his mount into the forest. The light of moon and numberless stars vanished, plunging him into darkness. Overhead, branches met to form a whispering roof that obliterated the sky completely. The path wound through the forest, dotted here and there with small cottages belonging to the keeper of the woods and the few wood-choppers allowed to cull dead or dying trees. It was not these respectable cottages that interested Macheath, however. Deeper in the forest were to be found less-respectable haunts — shacks belonging to poachers, temporary hiding places for highwaymen and other lawbreakers.

Red Perkins, a poacher who sold his stolen game to Rooney, lived in one of them. With a memory of those two IOUs bearing Perkins's name, Macheath felt Perkins was in no position to balk if McGinty demanded a favor. The devil of it was, Macheath had no clear idea which shack it was. But he knew it was not far from the inn. He had been chatting with Rooney one day when Perkins came to sell him a bag of poached partridge.

"Where are they? Let's see them," Rooney had said.

"I didn't risk bringing them out of the forest till I knew if you wanted them. I'll get them now. I'll be back inside an hour." Which meant the shack was not more than half an hour away on foot. Macheath could do it in much less on horseback, if he knew which direction to take. He dismounted and began searching the tree line for signs of a path. Before he had gone far, he found one. It was only a narrow footpath; better to leave his mount behind. It would be quieter on foot in any case.

Macheath was an old hand at this from his guerrilla days in the Peninsula. He moved with the stealthy grace of a jungle cat, hardly disturbing a twig as he went forward. Were it not for the lump of cold fear in his stomach, he would have enjoyed it. But the desperate realization that they had Marianne drove him nearly to the edge of panic. He had to force himself to keep a steady, quiet pace. He didn't want to arrive too breathless to deal with La Rue and McGinty, or too overwrought to think straight.

He peered left and right. The path split, one branch going east, one west. Perkins's stunt to confuse the game warden. Macheath chose the right path, which he soon realized was the wrong path. It led to a creek where Perkins could hop in to confuse the trail if hounds were following him. He quickly backtracked and took the left path. He felt sure he was on the way to Perkins's shack now — but was that where they had taken Marianne? Were they even now molesting her, as McGinty had tried last night at the inn? He moved faster, faster, the twigs snapping loudly underfoot now, but he didn't slow down. He couldn't, for he had seen a dull glow of light through the branches. Perkins's shack!

As he rushed forward, a single shot shattered the night. Macheath froze in his tracks, then forged on, his heart slamming against his ribs.

CHAPTER
SEVENTEEN

Marianne couldn't see where they were taking her, but it was not down the main staircase. It was a narrow set of steps. She could feel her toes banging against a wall when she kicked. She heard a door squeak open; not the front door. If it was the back way, though, it was odd she hadn't heard the sounds of the kitchen. She didn't hear any sound from the stable now that she was outdoors, either. Was there another door? After they had gone a few yards, they put her down and made her walk, over rough terrain, for perhaps a quarter of a mile. Sometimes she felt bushes touch her ankles, so they must be in a wood. The forest behind the inn, of course.

It was important to know where she was, because she had every intention of escaping and had to know her way back. She had to believe that or else succumb to the blind panic that was scratching at her brain. The most unnerving part of it all was that the men barely spoke. When they did, they said not a word that would betray their intentions.

Before leaving the inn, La Rue had said, "We didn't plan on cargo. Where'll we store her?"

"Perkins owes me. We'll use his shack."

"She'll be hard to handle on horseback."

"Take Jim Todd's rig," McGinty had said.

The names Perkins and Jim Todd meant nothing to Marianne, but clearly McGinty had a very rudimentary understanding of private property.

When they stopped, she was tied up wing and leg and dumped into the back of a wagon on top of a few inches of hay. The blanket was torn off. She saw she was in a clearing in the forest, with a path leading out into a dense growth of mature timbers. Branches whispered high overhead. In the clearing, a myriad of stars spangled the black sky. The smaller man pointed the pistol at her as the other one trussed her up more tightly. They didn't warn her against calling for help, but it was implicit in that round black muzzle pointing at her. When she was secured, they put the blanket over her again and the wagon bumped along for an indeterminate amount of time and distance.

She struggled with her bindings, but the more she pulled the tighter they became. Where were they taking her? What were they going to do with her? Was McGinty planning to wreak his revenge for last night? "I'll have you here on the floor, minx," he had said. Oh, Lord! She wished she had taken the pistol when John offered it to her. Or even that she had put the little knife in her pocket. But she hadn't. It was in her reticule, in her room. She should have let John shoot him when he wanted to last night. The smaller one was McGinty, she was sure of that. Likely the bigger man was La Rue.

At length, the wagon stopped. The men exchanged a few words then. She listened, trying to hear them and, if possible, to recognize the other voice.

"The shack's dark. Perkins ain't home," La Rue said.

"He'd be out filling his jiggle bag. He don't lock his door."

"I'll take her in. You take the note to the duchess," one of them said. It wasn't McGinty's voice. She had never heard that voice before.

"Tomorrow'll be time enough."

"Don't be daft. Macheath might be back by then."

"I'll stay with the wench. You take the note." That was Dirty Dick.

"Do as I say, Dick. Kidnapping's bad enough. If we harm the lass, the law will never stop looking till they find us. You can buy all the girls you want after this is over."

"How much do we ask for?"

"The old malkin is good for thousands. Ask for five thousand — in cash."

"She wouldn't have that much on her."

"There's banks, ain't there? Tell her five thousand in cash tomorrow at noon."

"Where?"

There was a longish silence. "Nay, that'll never fadge. She'll send for Macheath. He could be back by noon, easy. Tell her the jewels, tonight. The groom brings them to the forest. The little groom — alone."

"That'd be Tom."

"Just say Tom brings them to the forest, and we'll find him."

Dick grumbled a bit, then left on foot.

She was hauled over the bigger man's shoulder like a sack of oats and carried into a cottage of some sort. A shack, they had called it. La Rue — she assumed he was La Rue — dumped her on to what felt like a horsehair sofa, all hard and lumpy, and threw the blanket over her. She managed to ease the gag from her mouth and breathed the warm moist air smelling of horse which was trapped under the blanket. She waited and listened. He was pouring himself a drink. She hoped he didn't get drunk and forget the warning he had given McGinty.

At least she hadn't been left alone with Dirty Dick. She began working at her bindings again. They were some rough sort of hemp that scratched her wrists. If only she had brought her scissors with her. Was there nothing she could use? Then she thought of the nail file. She had dropped it into her pocket earlier. It would take time, but it might eventually work through the hemp.

By squirming she could get her hand over to the side pocket of her skirt. She slid her fingers in and managed to get the thin blade between her thumb and forefinger. The more difficult part was reaching the rope when her hands were tied together. She got a tight grip on the end of the file and began to saw. The strokes were short, due to her hands being tied together. She had to work carefully to prevent the movement of the blanket from revealing what she was doing.

She heard a bottle rattle against the table. Another drink was poured into the glass. He drank and smacked his lips, then walked across the room. From the sounds that followed, she thought he was building up the fire in the grate. It was stifling under the blanket, but it would be chilly in the room. Where were they? No sounds other than those made by the man could be heard. It was an isolated cottage somewhere in the woods. Impossible to find! She kept sawing at the ropes as these thoughts raced through her mind.

At least the man didn't show any interest in her as a woman. Just as she was thanking God for this mercy, she heard heavy steps approaching the sofa. He stopped when he reached it. She held her breath, praying as she had never prayed before in her life. She felt his hand on the blanket. He lifted it and stared down at her. He had removed his mask, and she saw a tall man with rough reddish hair and snuff-brown eyes, red around the rims. His hands were the size of ham hocks. She had never seen him before.

He gave a snort, said, "I don't know what he sees in you," and dropped the blanket back over her face. She never imagined she would be so glad to be found unattractive. The man returned to the table and his drink, and Marianne to her work with the nail file. It seemed a hopeless task. She could not get a firm hold on the smooth ivory handle. It kept slipping, but she persevered, as she couldn't think of anything else useful to do. After perhaps a quarter of an hour, she had severed one strand of the rope. When she pulled, the rest of it came loose. Her hands were free. That small success gave her confidence and courage. Her hands were numb. She flexed her fingers to restore the flow of blood.

Now if she could get her feet loose without alerting him what she was about! She rolled over, turning her back to the room to allow herself a little freedom of movement. When the man didn't say anything, she began working her hands down to her ankles. It was easier to untie the ropes there than to cut through them. After a few broken fingernails, the rope at her feet was loose. She was no longer bound, but she was still locked in a house with a large man holding a gun. A man who was rapidly drinking himself into drunkenness.

She turned over quietly until she was facing the room again and listened. The only sound was the snapping of wood in the grate and the occasional rattle of a glass or bottle on the table. She risked lifting the corner of the blanket and peeking out. La Rue sat at the table, facing her but not looking at her. He was looking at the fire. When he rose to go and stoke it, she lowered the blanket and looked around the room for a weapon. He had left his pistol on the table. Could she reach it before he caught her? If she failed, the attempt might jolt him into an ugly mood — and with a fair bit of liquor in him, God only knew what revenge he might take.

She wanted something closer to hand. There was nothing. The place was only a one-room shack, with no stove or sink. The man who lived here must cook at the hearth. If he washed, it could only be in a nearby creek. La Rue was bent over the fire, working at it with a poker. He held a log in his hand, preparing a spot to add it to the fire. That would take him half a minute at least. She might not have another chance. She'd make a dart for his gun.

She pushed the blanket aside and leapt toward the table. She didn't look behind her, but she heard La Rue drop the log.

"Here!" he shouted, and came after her.

Her fingers closed over the weapon. It was heavy and felt awkward. She had never fired a gun in her life, but she knew she had to pull the trigger. She turned and saw him coming toward her, wearing an ugly scowl.

"If you come one step closer, I'll shoot," she said, surprised at the firmness of her voice. She had thought it would quake with the terror she felt. Her hand was trembling. She saw La Rue look at it, and his lips drew back, revealing crooked, yellowed teeth.

"It ain't loaded," he said.

Staring into his snuff-brown eyes, she couldn't see any shadow of fear. Surely he hadn't gone to rob the duchess with an unloaded gun.

"Yes, it is," she said, and put her other hand on the gun handle to steady it.

"Try it," he said, his lips stretching into an evil grin.

His eyes held hers, neither of them wavering. It was a battle of wills. She gritted her teeth and determined that if he came one step closer, she'd pull the trigger and hope he had been bluffing about the gun's not being loaded.

He took a step toward her. She steadied the pistol as well as her trembling hand allowed, aimed at his right shoulder to avoid striking his heart, and pulled the trigger. The explosion reverberated in the small room, sounding as if a cannon had gone off. It rang and echoed in her ears. The man stared at her in astonishment, emitted a grunt, and fell slowly to the floor. She dropped the gun and stood a moment, gathering her wits, then she ran toward the door. As she opened it, a low moan came from the man's throat. She stopped and turned back. The man was looking at her wildly.

"Help me, miss," he said in a weak voice. "I'm bleeding to death."

She saw the blood spreading down his left sleeve and found she could not leave him to die by inches. Slowly, reluctantly, she turned and went back to him.

"Have a look at my wound," he said. "See if you can stop the flow of blood."

She bent down and reached to open his shirt. He sat up like a jack-in-the-box. His right hand clamped her wrist and wrenched her arm back until she was afraid he'd break it. "Shoot me, will you, wench? I know what to do with the likes of you!" he said in a firm, angry voice. It had all been an act. His wound was only a scratch. He stood up and dragged her to her feet, with her arm still cruelly twisted behind her back.

She couldn't fight anymore. She wasn't strong enough to overpower a big man. She wasn't evil enough to deal with such people as this on their own terms.

"If you wasn't so ugly, I'd take you myself. You're only fit for the likes of McGinty," he scoffed.

He shoved her back toward the sofa, where the ropes and blanket awaited her. She couldn't face it again. Something inside her revolted. She had one free hand. She slid it into her pocket and drew out the nail file. When he released her arm to shove her on to the sofa, she turned and struck at his face with the nail file. It cut a slash into his cheek. Blood spurted. While he instinctively reached to feel it, she turned and bolted for the door, with the man in hot pursuit, cursing her. She had her fingers on the doorknob when he caught her by her hair and yanked her back.

She watched in growing desperation as the door-knob turned and the door flew open. McGinty was back, to have his way with her. But it was not McGinty who came in. It was Macheath, with a menacing smile on his face and blood in his eye.

"I have been wanting to do this for a long time," he said as his fist flew out and La Rue dropped to the floor.

Marianne ran into his arms and buried her head in his shoulder. She couldn't speak. She didn't even want to open her eyes. She just wanted the safety of his arms around her, holding her tight.

CHAPTER
EIGHTEEN

"Are you all right, my dear?" Macheath asked a moment later, when she had stopped trembling.

She looked up at him with wide, dazed eyes. "I shot him, John."

"Good!"

"I thought he was dying, but it was only a ruse to get me to stay."

"My sweet innocent," he said ruefully, "how did you come to fall into such company as this?"

"It all started when you held up the duchess's coach," she said, not reproachfully, but merely answering his question. Macheath swallowed a lump in his throat and she continued. "I don't suppose you recovered the diamonds?"

"I know where they are. I beat it out of McGinty."

La Rue squinted and frowned, but didn't ask for McGinty's whereabouts. "I'm bleeding. I need help," he said.

"Don't pay him any heed!" Marianne said. "It is a trick, John. Tie him up and let us leave."

"He's not going anywhere," Macheath replied. He picked up La Rue's gun and led Marianne out into the darkness with his arm around her shoulder, holding her to his side.

Outside, he tossed the gun into the forest. Then he tilted her face up to his. It was pale in the moonlight.

"If anything had happened to you, I — Oh, Marianne! This is all my fault. I am so sorry, darling." He drew her into his arms and hugged her fiercely. "You were right. Turning highwayman is not the way to solve the world's problems. When I went back upstairs and saw you gone, I — They drugged Miguel, you see, which is how it happened."

"I thought it was you at the door and let them in."

"We should have arranged a signal. I was sure they wouldn't come until later. Was it very bad?"

"Yes, it was horrid. And the worst part was finding out that I could be just as bad as they were. I never thought I could shoot anyone in cold blood. I can well understand now how the war made you so vicious." Macheath winced. "Oh, John, I didn't mean — You were always quite civil to the duchess and me."

"I know you didn't mean it. That is the worst part of it all. You were simply telling the truth. I have become a brute without realizing it."

"But a gentlemanly brute," she said consolingly and changed the subject. "That man I shot in the arm is La Rue, is he?"

"Yes," he replied distractedly, for his mind lingered on what she had inadvertently said, "vicious."

"Where's McGinty?" she asked.

"Tied to a tree a little farther along. He came creeping up behind me as I was running toward the shack. I used his kerchief to tie him by the wrists to a sapling."

As they continued, Marianne related her night's suffering. Each of her torments caused another stab of guilt for Macheath. To have subjected an innocent young girl to such horrendous doings was unconscionable.

Not far along the path they came to McGinty, tied to a sapling as Macheath had said. McGinty had given up trying to loosen his bonds. He scowled at them. "Ain't you going to release me?" he asked.

"Not until I see if you were telling me the truth about the diamonds," Macheath replied and continued on his way.

"Is La Rue dead?"

"Perhaps," Macheath called back and kept on walking. An echo of curses followed them.

When they came to the part of the path where he had tethered his mount, he helped Marianne up and she held on to his waist, her head resting against his back while they rode through the forest to the inn.

Once there, he hopped down and held out his arms. Marianne jumped into them and he swung her to the ground. He kept his arms around her a moment, enjoying the feel of her tiny waist.

"You can let me go now, John," she said primly.

"I can, but I don't want to." She stepped back. "Go upstairs and see if the duchess is still sleeping," Macheath said. "I'll be up in half an hour."

He rode to the next signpost, and there, hidden under a rock as McGinty had said, sat the diamonds, wrapped in a handkerchief. He slipped them into his pocket, rode back to release McGinty, and went to the inn.

Marianne found the duchess still sleeping soundly, oblivious to the horrors of the night. She closed the door and went into the next room to tidy herself. Her hair hung in strands around her shoulders. She was covered in dust and dirt from the wagon. Her wrists were sore and her fingernails a mess, but when she looked in the mirror, she saw a smiling, confident woman.

A downtrodden girl, frightened of her own shadow, had set out on this trip expecting no more than a tedious journey with a short respite in London for the wedding. And instead she had had a life-changing adventure. She had met a highwayman, been nearly drowned, been kidnapped, and shot a man. But she had survived it all. She would never be the same again, never frightened of a foolish old woman just because she had a title. And best of all, she had fallen in love. Bath would be desperately dull after this.

When the tap came at the door later, she felt a spurt of fear and didn't open it until she called, "Who is it?"

"It's me, John."

Then she opened the door. He came in, dangling the diamonds from his fingers. In the dull glow from the grate, they hardly sparkled. They might have been made of paste.

"What a lot of bother these bits of crystalline carbon have caused," he said, and dropped the necklace into her fingers. "One day you'll have a set of your own."

"I don't share the duchess's love of showy baubles."

"How much of what has happened tonight do we tell the old girl?" he asked. "You will want to spare her the more gruesome details, I expect."

"Why should I? She has never spared me. Let her realize the mischief she has caused."

"Actually, I am the one who has caused the harm, which you kindly call mischief. And with her heart, you know . . ."

"Yes, we must take that into account, of course. Very well, I shall tell her La Rue came while she was asleep, and you recovered the diamonds as we planned. I do think, though, that people ought to be accountable for their actions."

Macheath took this unusually stern speech as a reflection on his own part in the affair. Gazing at Marianne, he did not see the frightened girl who had cowered in his arms, trembling, an hour ago.

"Did you release McGinty?" she asked.

"Yes. He'll tend to La Rue's bullet wound."

"They should both be reported to the constable."

Macheath didn't reply, just looked at her uncertainly. She knew how he felt about that. They had discussed it. He was equally culpable, as far as that went. Did she think he should be reported as well? It was not the moment for romance. He deduced that Marianne was having second thoughts about all this, about him. Her sufferings over the past days were taking their toll. From the mutinous set of her chin, he judged it would not be long before they were arguing if he stayed. And really he had not much to say in his own defense. He had foolishly tried to right a country's wrongs single-handedly. A childish, quixotic thing to do. Better to let her cool down and talk to her in the morning.

"I'll let you get a few hours' sleep," he said.

She brushed a weary hand over her forehead, revealing the scrapes and bruises on her wrists. "Who could sleep after a night like this?"

"You'll want to tend to those scrapes. And a glass of wine to help you rest."

"I'll have some of that brandy in water."

He wanted to clear the air before leaving. "Marianne, I'm truly sorry."

"I know. I know, John," she said brusquely. With her newfound confidence, she added, "But it was really very bad of you. The duchess never did you any harm."

"I know. I'll call on her tomorrow and apologize."

He wanted to kiss her, but she looked too daunting. "Until tomorrow, then," he said, and left with a last long, searching gaze.

Marianne poured a glass of water and added a dollop of brandy to it. She sat alone by the smoldering grate, sipping and thinking until she felt her eyelids grow heavy; then she went to bed. She slid the diamonds under her pillow for safekeeping.

She slept until eight o'clock and awoke to find the duchess standing over her. For the first time in memory, the duchess had tidied her own hair.

"Wake up, sleepyhead! We were supposed to meet Macheath downstairs. What happened last night? Did he get my diamonds?"

Marianne shook herself awake. She reached under her pillow and handed the duchess the necklace. Her faded face creased into smiles.

"Good lad! Why did you not awaken me, Marianne? You know I wanted to see the scoundrel who robbed me."

"You were sleeping so soundly we decided to let you have your rest."

"That was well done of Macheath. Very thoughtful to let me build up my resources for the trip to London. I shall go downstairs and thank him in person. Join us as soon as you make yourself decent." Her sweeping gaze took in Marianne's rough hands and wrists. "You ought to put some Gowlands Lotion on those hands, Marianne, and file your fingernails. A lady is judged by her hands, you know."

She dropped the necklace into her reticule and bustled off to meet her new beau. Marianne made a hasty toilette and went downstairs. She found the unlikely couple enjoying their breakfast of gammon and eggs, laughing and joking like old friends.

"This scoundrel is up to all the rigs," the duchess told Marianne. "When La Rue pretended he didn't have my diamonds, Macheath shot him in the arm. That is the way to deal with these villains. I like a man who knows how to handle himself. You will go far in London, Macheath."

"Is it arranged that Macheath will be settling in London?" Marianne asked.

"Why, we have practically settled on an heiress for him," the duchess crowed. She was in prime humor, with a handsome young buck exerting himself to please her and her necklace once again back around her neck, hidden by her gown. She had given the maid the paste pearls in lieu of the customary tip.

Macheath cast an apologetic smile at Marianne for that remark about having found him an heiress.

"Lord Boucher's youngest gel, Lady Amelia," the duchess continued. "She has only ten thousand, but excellent connections. Connections are not to be ignored. Boucher can put a dozen court appointments in your way, Macheath, and she is not a bad-looking lass, either, bar the platter face. She was in Bath a year ago visiting her aunt. You didn't meet her, Marianne. I saw her at the assembly rooms one evening."

She continued in this vein while Marianne ate a little breakfast. She noticed it was no longer an undemanding cit's daughter but a lord's with a hefty dowry that was spoken of as his future wife. That might very well tempt Macheath into agreeing. She found it hard to swallow. He was going along with the duchess's scheme, asking in a playful way what the Boucher girl was like and what court appointments she might bring him.

They left half an hour later. Macheath accompanied them on his mount, as agreed upon. He traveled sometimes in front and sometimes behind. When they reached the western edge of London, he joined them and rode alongside the carriage. The duchess lowered her window.

"It is *au revoir* for now, Macheath. Thank you for your escort. I shall expect you to call on me at

Grosvenor Square in two days' time. Say goodbye to Macheath, Marianne. I told him he could leave us when we reached London. Nothing will befall us here in broad daylight."

Marianne put her head to the window. She wore a questioning look. She had not had a moment alone with him since last night. And as she considered it, Macheath had been rather cool all day. All this talk of Lady Amelia was upsetting. If Macheath planned to abandon his life of crime, he would require a patron to establish himself. If Lady Amelia was pretty, he would easily be seduced into offering for her.

"Goodbye, Macheath," she said with a questioning look, hoping for some word, some sign to assuage her worries. With the duchess at her elbow, she couldn't call him John, as she wanted to.

"It is not goodbye. It is *au revoir*, Miss Harkness. I shall see *you* the day after tomorrow as well."

Then he tipped his hat, turned his mount around, and rode off, back the way they had come. Marianne had the most awful, sinking sensation she would never see him again.

CHAPTER
NINETEEN

All her life, Marianne had wanted to visit London. It loomed in her mind as a fairyland full of unimagined splendor: kings and queens, princes and princesses, castles and grand mansions with gold domes. But at the outskirts of the city, what she surveyed through the carriage window was the sprawling shambles of a million people. The roads were rough, and shabby cottages jostled cheek by jowl with manufactories and warehouses. Ragged urchins stood with their hands out, begging. There were more donkey carts and farm wagons and pedestrians than carriages. They had to crawl at a snail's pace for half a mile behind a drover with his herd of cattle. Accustomed to the serene elegance of Bath, she felt they must have come to the wrong place.

More elegant houses and an occasional church appeared as they drew closer to polite London. From the carriage window she saw a stretching meadow dotted with trees and bushes and was informed by Her Grace that she was looking at the world-famous Hyde Park. The carriage turned onto Park Lane, where fine mansions of gray or brown brick, all looking similar in size and style, lined the wide cobble-stoned pavement.

Here everything was ordered and beautiful but not overwhelming to a young lady from Bath. She had expected more, and was well aware that there was more, but she did not see it today. They drove directly to Grosvenor Square, where they entered one of the brown brick houses with white pillars guarding a pedimented door of oak.

A rattle of the brass-wreath knocker brought an aged butler to admit them.

"Your Grace," he said, standing aside to usher them into a hallway paved with liver-colored marble, and thence into a dark, dismal purple saloon, where a replica of the duchess sat by an enormous grate in which an exceedingly small fire smoldered. She had an embroidery frame beside her and a fat white poodle at her feet. This dame was Lady Thornleigh, a countess and younger (by two years) sister of the duchess. The only discernible difference between them was that Belle was about twenty pounds heavier. She had her sister's trick of spending very little of her money on either candles or coal, so that her mansion was dark and frigid. She wore two shawls, a gray one around her shoulders and a black one over her knees.

The ladies brushed cheeks and said, "How do you do, dear?" as if they met every day, though Marianne knew they had not seen each other for over five years. Marianne was presented, examined, and given approval. As soon as this was done, she was told to run upstairs and see to the duchess's unpacking, but first fetch her shawl — her woolen shawl, mind. A servant led her up a wide, dark staircase to a long, dark hallway, into a surprisingly bright but cold bedchamber. She took down the shawl and returned abovestairs, where she kept herself busy and tried to keep herself warm unpacking the duchess's trunk and arranging her own belongings in a smaller room next door until she was called down to tea.

It was difficult to imagine how Lady Thornleigh had put on those extra pounds, for her tea was parsimonious in the extreme. Plain bread and butter and marmalade and tea were all she served. The ladies were joined by an elderly gentleman called Sir Gervase Horne, who flirted discreetly with the noble dames and ate most of the bread and butter. The poodle, Bingo, was given all the crusts. Gervase brought them invitations to a party that evening in honor of the bridal couple. Marianne's hopes soared, then fell to the ground again when the duchess decided she was too fagged after the journey and would stay home. Lady Thornleigh thought it looked dreadfully like rain. As she disliked to have the horses put to in the rain, she would remain at home as well.

The sisters and Marianne had dinner at seven-thirty in a drafty dining room, where the conversation was as dull as the food. Over mutton and turbot in white sauce, they discussed people from their youth, names Marianne had never heard. Most of them seemed to be dead. The cause of their demise was of great interest to the octogenarians. At eight-thirty they retired to the purple saloon. At nine o'clock tea was served, and at nine-thirty they retired to their beds.

In the morning, Lady Thornleigh mentioned going to Bond Street to buy new gloves for the wedding. Again Marianne allowed herself to hope, but as the sky was gray her hostess decided against having the horses put to and sent a footman instead. To keep her "amused," Marianne was given a tangled wad of colored embroidery woolens to separate, and she sat at this chore while the sisters entertained a few relatives. One of the duchess's daughters came, not Eugenie but Hortense. Eugenie was too busy with wedding details.

Strangely, the duchess did not mention the troubles she had encountered on her journey. When her daughter inquired, she said only that a bridge had failed them, and a nice gentleman had helped them escape drowning. Neither her daughter nor her sister was curious enough to inquire for his name. Sir Gervase paid a brief visit in the afternoon and again ate most of the bread and butter, even the crusts, which put Bingo into a snappish temper.

Marianne was sorely disappointed with her visit to fabled London. Were it not for her memories and her hopes, she would have been in the mopes. While the old ladies gossiped, her mind was back at the inn with Captain Macheath. He had said he would call. Perhaps he would come that evening. She imagined herself seeing the real London with him. She knew a highwayman would not be accepted in polite society, but she pictured herself at a ball with him, floating in a lovely silk gown that she did not, in fact, possess. Her hair was piled high on her head, and at her throat sparkled the diamonds she claimed were of no interest to her.

"Eh, Marianne?" the duchess said, interrupting her daydreams.

Marianne returned to reality with a guilty start. "Er, sorry, ma'am. I didn't hear you."

"Belle was saying you will want to have a jig with Gervase at the wedding. He is a widower, you know. An excellent *parti*. Not so young as he might be, of course, but there is plenty of life in him yet."

"Not young?" Lady Thornleigh said, lifting her eyebrows in astonishment. "He is not a day over fifty-five."

"Rubbish! He is sixty if he is a day."

"No, no. You remember he married in '81, the year Papa died, and everyone said he was too young to shackle himself with a bride. And she had no dowry to speak of, either. I remember perfectly, for we could not attend the wedding as we were in mourning."

"That wasn't Gervase. It was Cousin Lloyd. He married the Rafferty girl — an Irish chit, but with a hefty dowry."

They were off on another ramble down memory lane, and Marianne's thoughts returned to greener pastures. When she had hoped to meet an undemanding gentleman, it was not some widower old enough to be her grandpapa. She sat with one ear cocked, hoping every time she heard the door knocker sound that the butler would enter to announce, in a disapproving voice, "Captain Macheath." It didn't happen. Relatives and friends aplenty dropped in to gossip about the wedding, but they all had either gray or white hair except a Lord Penniston, who had no hair at all on his head but a fair-size bush growing out of his ears.

With a wedding to look forward to in the morning, the ladies retired at nine that evening.

The wedding was to take place at two o'clock the next afternoon in St. George's, Hanover Square, with a reception at the groom's papa's mansion in Park Lane after. The mansion on Grosvenor Square was all aflutter. The sisters were busy comparing toilettes, worrying whether an egret fan was too lavish or the painted chicken skin too common.

"I shall wear my emerald pin on my turban," Lady Thornleigh explained. "The chicken-skin fan does not really go with emeralds."

"I shall take my painted parchment fan," the duchess said. "It is not stylish, but it gives a wonderful breeze, and you know how hot the duke keeps his saloon. As bad as Carlton House. I should hate to pay his heating bills."

"Oh, as to giving a breeze, I find my ivory fan —"

"Ivory! The very thing, Belle. Elegant but not showy. Ivory is at home anywhere."

Knowing she would be required to assist the duchess with her toilette, Marianne arranged her own early. Mercifully, the blue slippers that matched her gown had not been ruined during her adventures. When she slid the silk stockings on, she felt quite like a lady of leisure. Her blue gown was simple, but its color suited her. With it she wore her mama's pearls, which she had hidden in the pocket of her best petticoat to escape the highwayman and forgotten all about until she required them. She drew her curls into a nest on top of her head and fastened them in place with half a dozen pins, which she knew would give her a headache before the party was over, but it would be worth it.

Her toilette was as fine as she had ever worn when she went below to ask if Her Grace was ready to begin dressing. Her face was pale, though, from waiting and worrying. She was afraid the duchess would rag at her for looking so stylish, but neither of the sisters noticed her improved appearance.

Wedding or no, the duchess never wore anything but black. Her gown was of silk, however, smuggled in from France. The diamonds looked well with it. She wore a fond smile as Marianne hung them around her crepe-like throat.

"I wonder if we shall ever see him again," she said in a dreamy voice. Not the Captain, not Macheath, but *him*, as if he had been preying on her mind, too.

"He said he would call," Marianne reminded her. Was it possible the duchess had forgotten?

"So he did. I very much doubt we shall see him. I could see he was not really interested in Lady Amelia. He never asked a single question about her looks. Even in a marriage of convenience, a gentleman always inquires for a lady's looks. He only played along to amuse me. A sad rattle like Macheath would have no use for a lady. I expect the moping face you have worn these two days is in his honor. Forget him, Marianne. He is too dashing for you. You are in London now. You want to forget him and enjoy it."

Sorting woolens was no more exciting in London than in Bath, but Marianne didn't say so. She was afraid if she mentioned the promised tour the duchess would say Sir Gervase would escort her, and she had already decided she would as lief stay at home. Sir Gervase had begun casting sheep's eyes at her. She hoped to meet someone more agreeable at the wedding. And even if she didn't, the Prince Regent and two princesses were to attend. That would be something!

At two o'clock, Lady Thornleigh's ancient black carriage with the lozenge on the door drew up in front of the house on Grosvenor Square. Marianne felt a tingling excitement as the liveried footman helped her up the stairs into it. The long-awaited day had arrived, and she tried very hard to forget John and enjoy it, but she was dreadfully aware of an aching emptiness inside that had not been there before.

Unfamiliar with London, she anticipated a long drive through fashionable streets and was disappointed when the carriage stopped after only three blocks. This trip did not take half an hour by any means. By leaving home early, Lady Thornleigh achieved her aim of sparing her team the excitement of heavy wedding traffic, though Marianne did enjoy a glimpse of a few elegant rigs drawn by blood teams. The ladies entered the Corinthian portico into St George's, where a few eager guests sat waiting. The ladies were escorted halfway up the aisle and shown into a pew. The duchess planted herself firmly on the aisle seat and didn't budge. The other guests sharing her pew had to scramble in over her legs.

She gave Marianne a sharp poke in the ribs when Prince George and his two sisters strutted up the aisle. It would be wrong to say Marianne was disappointed in the prince. He was certainly an elegant figure; it was just that there was so much of him. His portly person was encased in blue satin and bedecked with ribbons and medals enough to impress a maharaja. The royal sisters were undistinguished as to either face, figure, or fashion. They would have been right at home in Bath. They looked like a couple of frumpy provincial matrons.

The bride was a vision of loveliness and the groom another disappointment. He was a pale, chinless, slender young gentleman who looked frightened to death. A wedding always appeals to the ladies, and with the prince, two princesses, and more tiaras than could be counted, Marianne was well enough entertained. She knew it was impossible that Macheath could be there, but she found her eyes searching the fashionable throng for him while the traditional vows were exchanged.

When the ceremony was over, the couple and their guests went in a cavalcade to Berkeley Square, another trip of only a few streets, but all of the scenery along the way was most elegant. The duke's house, the guests, the rich and plentiful feast all were as Marianne had been imagining. It was the largest and most exquisite party she had ever attended or could hope to attend. Once she was close enough to the prince to touch him.

She was excited, but still she could not seem to be happy. She was very much aware that she was an outsider here. If she had only one friend, one special someone, it would make it complete. She didn't know any of these people, who all seemed to know one another. She looked and listened as if she were attending a theater performance.

She remained with the duchess and was presented to a few aging people who smiled dismissively at her when they heard the words "my companion". She kept thinking about Macheath, how much more handsome he was than any of the grand noblemen who were here, talking and laughing too loudly and drinking too much of the duke's champagne.

In the evening, they were led to the ballroom. The duchess and Lady Thornleigh headed directly to the gilded chairs around the room's perimeter and had soon gathered a group of their coevals around them. Sir Gervase was the youngest person there, other than herself. After half an hour's conversation, he turned to Marianne and said, "Would you care to stand up with me, Miss Harkness?"

Tired of sitting, she accepted. He was a good dancer, but more importantly, he introduced her to a few people younger than eighty. One of them was even younger than Sir Gervase. Mr Thompson was a sprig of forty. He had been the groom's tutor and remained his friend. He had been rewarded with a living on one of the ducal estates. While the least demanding of spinsters would not have called him handsome, he was by no means ugly. His brown hair had very little gray in it. His nose was not so very long, and his eyes were quite nice. He was exactly the sort of gentleman Marianne had hoped to meet. He seemed to like her, but she did not go an inch out of her way to attach him. She had lost her taste for mere eligibility in a husband. After her dealings with Macheath, she demanded more.

She had the cotillion with Mr Thompson, and when it was finished he said, "The waltzes are next. I daresay no one would notice if we stood up together again. I own I feel a little out of my league here amongst so many titles." He did not say, but it was implicit in his manner, that he realized she, too, was out of her league.

"I'm sorry. I don't waltz," she said.

"Perhaps later, another set?"

"Thank you, Mr Thompson. I would enjoy it." It was better than sitting with the oldsters. They remained on the floor talking during the short intermission.

"Have you seen much of London yet?" he asked.

When she said she had not, he spoke until the musicians returned of the various sights she might enjoy seeing, then he took her back to the duchess, where Marianne sat, watching the waltzers.

She was not looking at the doorway when he arrived. It was Sir Gervase who spotted him and said, "There is young Lord Fortescue. He was not at the wedding, was he?"

Marianne looked and her heart gave a leap. It was him! But it was impossible! What could Macheath possibly be doing at the Season's most stylish wedding — unless he had come to rob the guests, and he was not wearing his mask. He wore a mulberry velvet jacket

184

and gray pantaloons. In the fall of immaculate lace at his throat, a ruby glowed richly.

"Fortescue, you say?" the duchess asked sharply, staring with narrowed eyes at the new arrival.

"Aye," Sir Gervase said. "He was in Spain with Wellington when his uncle stuck his spoon in the wall. Quite a hero, they say. We all thought he would make a name for himself in Parliament and amongst the ladies when he returned, but he makes himself pretty scarce. His uncle left the estate in a shambles I expect, and Fortescue is busy shoring up the cracks."

"He has come spying out a well-dowered bride," Lady Thornleigh said approvingly.

"Fortescue, you say?" the duchess repeated.

"Aye, his estate is close by," Gervase told her. "Fernwood is just a few miles west of London. I see him at a ball or the theater from time to time."

"Oh yes, Fernwood. It is on the other side of Chertsey, is it not?" she asked in a casual manner.

"That's it," he said, nodding. "A great old Gothic heap. I used to hunt there when his uncle was alive."

While they discussed him, Marianne stared in disbelief. Her highwayman was a lord! Rather than cheering her, this news was a crushing blow. A reformed highwayman might marry her, but a lord! He had come to spy out a fortune, as Lady Thornleigh had said. She watched with an aching heart as he looked all around the room, from one pretty lady to another. Then he turned his gaze toward the gilded chairs around the edge of the room, examining each face until he saw the duchess.

185

A small smile lifted his lips. His gaze continued until he saw Marianne. Then he began to walk purposefully toward her.

CHAPTER
TWENTY

Marianne had the strange sensation that she was suffocating. She heard excited voices echoing around her but had no idea what they were saying. Every atom of her attention was riveted on John. The voices were a mere babble in the background, until a sharp pinch on the arm jarred her to attention.

"Don't say a word. Let me do the talking," the duchess hissed in her ear. The command was unnecessary. Marianne could not have spoken if her life depended on it.

In seconds, Macheath was standing in front of her, bowing to the older ladies first, before allowing himself the pleasure of a close scrutiny of Marianne.

"Fortescue," Her Grace said, allowing him to take her hand. "Speak of the devil. We were just talking about you. I was telling Lady Thornleigh how you rescued me when my carriage slid into the river."

"I am happy to see you looking so well, Your Grace." His eyes just flickered to the diamonds. The duchess patted them and smiled. Then he turned again to Marianne. "And you, Miss Harkness."

"This is my sister, Lady Thornleigh," the duchess continued. He bowed to Lady Thornleigh and Sir Gervase.

"Nice to see you, Fortescue," Gervase said, nodding. "How is your mama? I did not see her at the wedding."

"She is at Fernwood, Sir Gervase. I shall tell her you were asking for her."

"I hope you are not planning to dart off to Fernwood immediately?" Her Grace said. "You recall we had some plans for you, Cap — Fortescue."

"Indeed I am not, ma'am. I shall do myself the honor of calling on you tomorrow, if you permit?" The duchess nodded graciously.

Having done the pretty with the oldsters, he could at last turn his full attention to Marianne. "May I have the pleasure of a waltz, Miss Harkness?"

"I don't waltz," she said in a stricken voice.

"The patronesses of Almack's would not approve," Sir Gervase mentioned.

This was enough to incite the duchess to objection. "I do not require Lady Jersey's approval!" she said at once. "If a young lady under my charge wishes to waltz at my great-granddaughter's wedding, she may do it."

"Aye, it is a private party after all," Sir Gervase said at once.

"But I don't know how to waltz," Marianne explained.

Macheath gave her an impatient look. "I'll teach you," he said, and taking her hand, he helped her from her chair and marched her out of the room into a lofty corridor where a few groups of guests stood talking. As they walked off, he said, "Really, Marianne! You made it demmed awkward to escape."

She turned to him and said, "Why did you lie to us?"

"If you are referring to my being Fortescue, you knew my name wasn't really Macheath. You charged me with it some time ago."

"I didn't know you were a lord," she said accusingly.

"I felt it the wiser course to conceal my identity until I was away from the inn. A careless word could have been disastrous. If Bow Street ever tumbled to it that Fernwood was harboring a felon, it would have been embarrassing for Mama."

"What are you doing here?"

"Celebrating the nuptials of an old friend. I was invited! I was too late to get to the church, so I came here, looking for you. Why did you think I had come? To steal the ring off the bride's finger?"

"You need not worry the duchess will reveal your secret, milord."

"It is not the duchess I am worried about."

"I won't tell, either. No one would believe me if I did."

"Good. Now that we've got that sorted out, let us find some place to talk."

He took a crippling grip on her arm and led her at a lively gait down the corridor, past the ballroom to a door on the left. He peered into a small parlor and, finding it vacant, drew her inside and closed the door.

His dark eyes moved over her hair, her face, lingering on her lips. "I have come to claim my reward, Marianne," he said softly.

"You must speak to the duchess, but I doubt she will pay a reward for her diamonds, as you stole them in the first place."

When he replied, his voice had lost its softness and become impatient. "Have you suddenly lost the use of your wits, woman? Duchesses and diamonds have nothing to do with it. I have abandoned my life of crime as you recommended." His hands closed possessively over hers, drawing her closer to him. His dark eyes devoured her. "The reward I have come to claim is — you."

A tide of trembling joy surged inside her. She looked at him uncertainly and felt any future with him was impossible. He was too handsome, too dashing, too rich, and titled besides. Every heiress in the room would be after him. "But you're a lord!" she said.

"And you are a lady. I hope to make you my lady, Marianne. You know I love you. Will you marry me?"

"How can I marry you?" she asked angrily. "First you are too low — a common felon, and now you are suddenly a lord. Why can't you be a vicar or a — a clerk, or some such thing?"

He considered this absurdity a moment. "I was a soldier for a few years. Will that do?"

"You were probably a general," she said with another accusing look.

"A colonel was the highest rank I made. My dear, this is mere quibbling," he said with a shake of his head. "I am me, whatever title Society hangs on me. You know me better than most. You have seen the worst of me. Let me show you the better part."

"You must marry an heiress. Fernwood is falling apart, and I haven't a sou to my name."

A glinting smile flashed out. "We know how to take care of that, don't we? The roads will be thick with well-inlaid gentry returning home from this wedding."

"John! You mustn't even think of it!"

A well-feigned frown furrowed his brow. "Without a good woman to keep me on the right path, I fear I shall be lured back into that dangerous life."

After a pause she said, "Is Fernwood very derelict?"

"Falling apart," he lied.

"Really?" she said, smiling. "And the rents?"

"Every sou goes to pay off the mortgages. We shall have to live on my officer's half pay."

"I am rather good at skimping," she said consideringly.

"So I have observed. You have even skimped on giving me an answer."

"I should hate to think of you falling back into that dangerous life."

"Then you'll just have to marry me, won't you?" he said reasonably.

He palmed her cheeks with his warm hands, forcing her to look at him. He gazed into her eyes, glowing with hope and happiness. "Won't you?" he repeated in softly caressing tones, as his lips grazed hers.

Ripples of pleasure coursed along her veins. She tried to answer, but with his lips nibbling at hers, she managed only a soft "Mmmm . . ."

"I'll take that for a yes," he murmured, and drew her into his arms for a long, deep kiss.

Marianne felt her heart pounding against his hard chest. The masculine strength of him surrounded her, turning her knees to water and her blood to flames as his hungry kiss savaged her heart. An answering strength grew in her to match his need. She wrapped her arms around his neck and held him tightly. One hand moved higher and she ran her fingers through his crisp hair. How had she thought she could settle for a modest vicar or a dull clerk? This was life! This was love! Highwayman, soldier, lord — what did it matter? He was John, he loved her, and she loved him with a fierce, consuming passion she had never imagined herself capable of.

After a long embrace he released her. "I take it that was a yes?" he said huskily.

"Yes, John," she whispered.

"No ifs, no buts?"

"No. I'll marry you. I trust you, John."

"What a consummate strategist you are. How can I misbehave after that — or want to? And now we shall waltz."

"I can't waltz. I told you. I don't know how."

"Yes, you can. Just follow my lead," he said and brought her back to the ballroom with his hand holding her elbow in a possessive grip.

When he took her in his arms, she found the waltz magically easy. Their bodies were in harmony, moving together as effortlessly as a pair of swallows soaring in the blue. The trick was to not think but just abandon yourself to the music.

When the waltz was over, he returned her to the duchess.

"About time," Her Grace said. "My sister and I are ready to go home, Marianne. Say thank you to Lord Fortescue. Don't forget you are to call on me tomorrow, Fortescue."

"I shan't forget, Your Grace." His eyes turned to Marianne. "I look forward to it."

Sir Gervase soon joined them at Grosvenor Square.

"Young Fortescue caused quite a stir at the wedding," he said when they were settled in before the scanty fire in the grate with a cup of cocoa.

"Who was he standing up with when you left?" the duchess asked.

"He left when I did. He has opened his house on Manchester Square, as he was expecting some servants to arrive. The debs were disappointed at his leaving. He didn't stand up with anyone."

Marianne smiled to herself. He had stood up with her. When he asked the duchess for her hand, she would cease being nobody. After half an hour's discussion of the wedding, Gervase left and the sisters went up to bed.

As Marianne helped Her Grace undress, the duchess said, "I always knew Macheath was a gentleman. Did I not say so? Not a Fitz-Matthew as I thought, but a Fortescue. They are some kin, I believe. Odd he turned highwayman, for they were saying at the wedding that Fernwood is not mortgaged at all. He is pretty well to grass. It would be the war that gave him such fantastical notions. The right lady will settle him down. I shall arrange for him to meet some debs. I saw you looking very pleased with yourself when you were dancing with him, Marianne. You must not go getting any notions he cares for you. Don't fret about it. I have not forgotten your tour of London. Sir Gervase has kindly offered to show you St. Paul's and the Tower."

"Lord Fortescue has offered to show me London," Marianne said.

The duchess's eyebrows rose an inch. "Has he, indeed? That was kind of him. It is a mark of respect for myself, and perhaps to sweet-talk you into silence about his other life. Give those logs a shake, will you? This room is like an icehouse."

Marianne applied the poker to the grate and returned to her room, where she lay in bed for two hours before closing her eyes. She didn't care if Fernwood was a palace or a shambles. She would be there with John, and whatever sort of life awaited her, she could handle it.

When he called the next afternoon, he had a private word with the duchess. Her face was white with shock when she went abovestairs to speak to Marianne.

"You will not credit what I have to tell you, Marianne," she said. "I have just been speaking to Macheath." In her excitement, the old name came out. "He wants to marry you. You see what happens when you have the good fortune to be associated with a duchess. No doubt it was your proper behavior that attracted him. I have trained you well. I shall miss you," she said. Not a word was said about the possibility of Marianne refusing him.

"I offered to have the wedding at Bath," she continued. "He seems to think Fernwood would be better. His mama is poorly. She does not care for travel. I have no patience with invalids. She is still a youngster — sixty-something, I believe. If he got a special license, you could have the wedding while I am here — close enough to attend, I mean. As you are like a daughter to me, I should hate to miss your wedding. I always said we would find you a beau in London, did I not? I have done pretty well for you, if I do say so myself."

"I think I have done pretty well for myself, Your Grace," Marianne replied pertly. She was through with truckling and pulling her forelock.

The duchess gave her a rebukeful look, but when she spoke, her tone was more respectful. "We must have a good talk before the wedding, Marianne. There are things a young lady must know. Marriage is not all parties and new frocks. It has its duties as well."

"I am more familiar with duties than parties and new frocks, ma'am, as you know."

"So you are. Run along, then, before I change my mind. First he steals my diamonds, then my companion. What next?"

"Why, I think he has already stolen a corner of your heart, ma'am."

"Minx!"

Marianne ran downstairs to see John standing alone in the gloomy purple saloon, an elegant silhouette etched against the window. He was examining a small vermeil snuffbox. She took it from him and slapped his wrist.

"None of that, sir. You are a reformed thief."

He drew her into his arms, smiling tenderly. "Remind me why I reformed," he said, and took his reward.